"Why did you invite me?" she asked.

Joe regarded her from beneath his thick lashes. "Perhaps I was curious to see how far you intended to go."

Olivia stiffened. "Perhaps that's why I came, too," she declared coolly, refusing to let him see that he'd disconcerted her.

"You feel sorry for me, don't you, Mr. Castellano?"

"I don't feel sorry for you," he grated. "For myself, maybe." He raked back his hair with a hand that wasn't entirely steady. "Why are you doing this, Olivia? You're not really interested in me."

Her breath caught in her throat. "Aren't I?" she asked faintly, and then took a gulp of air when he uttered an oath and came toward her.

"Stop this!" he ordered angrily. "I don't know what the hell you think you're playing at, but I think you've forgotten I'm no green youth and you're definitely no *femme fatale!*"

ANNE MATHER began writing when she was a child, progressing through torrid teenage romances to the kind of adult romances she likes to read. She's married, with two children, and she lives in the north of England. After writing, she enjoys reading, driving and traveling to different places to find settings for new novels. She considers herself very lucky to do something that she not only enjoys, but also gets paid for.

Books by Anne Mather

Don't miss any of our special offers. Write to us at the following address for information on our newest releases.

Harlequin Reader Service
U.S.: 3010 Walden Ave., P.O. Box 1325, Buffalo, NY 14269
Canadian: P.O. Box 609, Fort Erie, Ont. L2A 5X3

ANNE MATHER

Pacific Heat

Harlequin Books

TORONTO • NEW YORK • LONDON
AMSTERDAM • PARIS • SYDNEY • HAMBURG
STOCKHOLM • ATHENS • TOKYO • MILAN • MADRID
PRAGUE • WARSAW • BUDAPEST • AUCKLAND

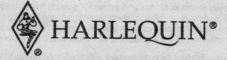

ISBN 0-373-12019-2

PACIFIC HEAT

First North American Publication 1999.

Copyright © 1998 by Anne Mather.

CHAPTER ONE

'DIANE HARAN!'

Olivia was stunned. Never in her wildest dreams had she ever expected to be offered such an assignment. To be invited to write Diane Haran's extraordinary rags-to-riches story was amazing. Diane Haran: screen goddess; model; superstar—and the woman who five years ago had walked off with Olivia's husband.

'Yes, Diane Haran,' repeated Kay Goldsmith, rather impatiently. 'You have heard of her, I suppose? Well, of course you have. Everybody has. She's world-famous. What is amazing about this is that Diane Haran should have heard of *you*.'

Olivia took a deep breath and stared at her agent. 'What do you mean? Diane Haran's heard about me?'

'Well, it was her idea that you should be the first to be offered the opportunity to be her biographer. She'd read your book about Eileen Cusack, I believe, and she'd obviously been impressed with your approach.'

'Really?'

Olivia knew she sounded cynical, but she couldn't help it. The theory that Diane Haran might have come up with the idea of asking her to be her biographer based on Olivia's interpretation of the Irish poet's tragic existence was laughable. Eileen Cusack had been a heroine in the truest sense of the word, balancing the needs of her family against a crippling bone-wasting disease, and writing some of the most beautiful lyrical verse besides. She'd died just a few weeks after her biography was published, but Olivia knew she would never forget her bravery or her sweetness.

Diane Haran was neither brave nor sweet. She was selfish

5

and manipulative and greedy. She'd been introduced to
Richard Haig at a party his agency had given for the then
rising star they'd hoped to represent. And, even though
she'd known he was married—Olivia had been at the party,
too, for heaven's sake—she hadn't hesitated about seducing
him away from his wife.

'Liv?'

Kay's curious enquiry brought Olivia's attention back to
the present and she realised she had been staring into space
for quite some time. But the idea that Diane Haran should
have suggested that she might want to play any part in her
biography was ludicrous, and it was time she explained that
to Kay.

'I can't do it,' she said, and when Kay's dark eyes widened in disbelief she pushed back her chair and got up from
the desk, crossing the room to stare out of the window.
Below Kay's office window, high in a tower block near the
embankment, the city traffic created a constant hum of
sound. But it was reassuring to know that life was going
on regardless. For a moment, she'd felt an awful sense of
time suspended.

'What do you mean, you can't do it?' Kay was on her
feet now, coming round the desk to join her at the window,
her plump, diminutive form accentuating Olivia's height
and the extreme slenderness of her figure. 'Have you any
idea what's on offer here? A fantastic fee, a share in the
royalties, and the chance to spend a few months in the sun.'

Olivia looked down at her companion. 'A few months in
the sun?' she echoed, compelled into an involuntary reply.

'That's right.' Kay explained. 'She wants you to go out
to California and spend some time with her. She's almost
through making her current movie and her agent says she'll
have some free time before the next one is due to start
shooting in September.'

Olivia's mouth was dry. 'Her agent?' she said faintly.

'Yes. Phoebe Isaacs, of the Isaacs and Stone agency. I
don't suppose you've heard of them, but they're pretty big

in the film business. Phoebe Isaacs is quite a tough cookie, as they say on the other side of the water.'

Olivia blinked. 'You're saying that this Phoebe Isaacs was the person who contacted you?'

'That's right.' Kay sensed the younger woman was weakening and attempted to press her case. 'But make no mistake, it was Diane Haran herself who chose this agency, because she knew you were one of my clients.'

Olivia blew out a breath. 'I still can't do it,' she said, even though her mind was buzzing with what Kay had just said. As far as she'd known, Richard was Diane's agent. That was the carrot she'd dangled in front of him all those years ago. As if her own undisputed beauty hadn't been enough.

'Why not?'

Kay was irritated, and Olivia couldn't really blame her. After all, the deal she was being offered was considerably more generous than anything she'd been offered thus far in her career. But then, her association with Kay was only three years old. Kay didn't know why she and her ex-husband had separated. It wasn't something she talked about these days, and when Richard had left her she'd still been working for the women's magazine she'd joined when she first left college.

'I just can't,' she insisted now, and, feeling slightly intimidated by Kay's frustration, she went back to the desk. 'You don't understand,' she added, pressing her hot palms down onto the cool wood. 'I—I've met Diane Haran. Years ago. And I didn't like her.'

Kay groaned. 'You don't have to *like* her!' she exclaimed, returning to her own side of the desk. 'And it's obvious she doesn't remember you. Or if she does—and if she knew how you felt—she doesn't hold any grudges. She wants you to write the story of how she became successful against all the odds. She's not looking for a lifelong commitment. Just a few short weeks of your time.'

Olivia licked her lips. The idea of flying out to

California, of spending several weeks, or even months, with Diane Haran, was anathema to her. It wasn't just that she disliked the woman. She hated her; she despised her. She blamed her totally for the break-up of her marriage. She and Richard had been happy together. Everyone had said they were the ideal couple. They'd known one another since their college days, and when Richard asked her to marry him she'd been in seventh heaven.

She hadn't been able to believe her luck, she remembered now, recalling how envious all her friends had been. Richard Haig had been the most attractive boy she'd ever seen, and one of the few people in her year who was actually taller than she was. At five feet ten, she'd always regarded her height as a drawback, but Richard had assured her he loved willowy women. The fact that she wasn't beautiful or outstandingly clever hadn't seemed to bother him either. For some reason, he had fallen in love with her, and she'd had no doubt that they'd live happily ever after...

'I can't do it,' she said again, aware that Kay was watching her closely. 'Kay, I'm flattered, but I'm sorry. This assignment just isn't for me.'

'You still haven't given me a decent reason why not,' retorted Kay, bumping down in her chair. 'Dammit, Liv, this is a chance of a lifetime. I can't let you throw it away.'

Olivia hesitated, and then sank down in her chair again. 'All right,' she said. 'I suppose I do owe you an explanation. I can't work for Diane Haran because I—*know*—the man she's married to—'

'Richard Haig?' Her ex-husband's name tripped carelessly off Kay's tongue, and Olivia made a concerted attempt not to show her surprise. 'Hey, you don't have to worry about that. From what I hear their marriage is on the rocks.'

Olivia swallowed. 'On the rocks?'

'So I hear.' Kay nodded. 'I gather they've been having problems for some time. He drinks, you know. Or at least that's the story. My guess is that some other man must have caught her eye.'

Olivia stared at her. 'I can't believe it.'

'Why not?' Kay was dismissive. 'You have to admit that this marriage has lasted longer than the other two she's had. Who was the first? Oh, yes, Gordon Rogers. She only lived with him for a couple of months.'

'I—I thought she'd only been married once—once before,' murmured Olivia faintly, but the woman opposite shook her head.

'No. Don't you remember that actor: Christian de Hanna? When she found out he was a needle-pusher, she threw him out.'

Olivia felt dazed. 'So—who is she seeing now?' she asked, trying to sound as if she was only casually interested, and Kay lay back in her chair with a rueful sigh.

'Search me,' she said. 'That's the million-dollar question. But you can be sure that he's got something your friend doesn't have.'

'My friend?'

For a moment, Olivia was confused, and Kay gave her a searching look.

'Richard Haig,' she said irritably. 'Our benefactor's current husband. If you want him, you can have him. Take my word for it.'

Olivia's lips parted. Was she so transparent? she wondered in dismay. With the little information she'd given Kay, had she exposed her feelings so clearly? 'I don't want him,' she declared hastily, but the words didn't sound convincing to her. The truth was, she did want him. She always had.

'Well, that's up to you,' said Kay briskly, evidently deciding she'd said enough. 'But I would seriously advise you not to turn this offer down. I don't think you realise the impact it could have, not just on the public but on your career. And goodness knows, you'd be in a position to pick up any number of other commissions at the same time.'

Olivia looked down at her hands, clasped together in her lap. She couldn't do this, she told herself fiercely, however attractive Kay was making it sound. She couldn't work with Diane Haran, not knowing what she'd done to Richard. And if Richard needed her he knew where to find her. It wasn't up to her to go looking for him.

But what if he was humiliated by what had happened? a small voice chided in her ear. What if he regretted the break-up of their marriage now, but was too ashamed of his own actions to approach her again? Richard had his pride, and their divorce had been rather acrimonious. He'd done his best to make her a scapegoat, and Olivia had been left feeling battered and bruised.

Which was another reason why she should refuse this commission, the same small voice reminded her sharply. Did she really want to lay herself open to that kind of emotional abuse again? And she wouldn't be working for Richard; she'd be working for Diane Haran. There was no guarantee that she'd even see him, if what Kay was saying was true. No matter how tempting it might be to imagine a reconciliation between them, she was thinking with her heart, not her head.

Realising Kay was waiting for her to say something, she asked the question that had first sprung into her mind. 'Why California?' she enquired. 'Doesn't she live in England any more?'

'I understand she has homes in both England and the United States,' said Kay immediately. 'Oh, and a villa in the South of France, as well. But as most of her films are made in America I suppose she finds it most convenient to live there.'

Olivia's mind boggled. She found it hard to conceive what it must be like to be so rich. Diane had probably found it hard, too, she acknowledged. At least, to begin with. A council flat in the East End of London was where she'd lived for the first fifteen years of her life.

'You'd have to do some research here,' Kay commented,

almost as if Olivia had agreed to her request. 'Her family have all moved away from Bermondsey, of course, thanks to Diane's generosity. But I expect there'll still be people there who remember her as a child. Schoolfriends, neighbours, and so on.'

Olivia regarded the other woman wryly. 'I do know how to go about researching a subject's background,' she remarked, wishing Kay would just let it go. But what she wished most of all was that Diane had never asked for her; had never ignited the spark of unwilling excitement that the thought of seeing Richard again could bring.

Kay had straightened in her chair now, and was watching her closely, and Olivia felt the heat from her thoughts invading the pale hollows of her throat. 'Does this mean you're thinking of accepting the commission?' Kay asked, leaning across her desk, and Olivia drew back from that avid stare.

'I—I have no desire to work with Diane Haran,' she insisted tensely, but they both knew that she hadn't actually said no.

Olivia got back to her flat in the late afternoon. Situated on the top floor of an old Victorian town house, the flat was her home and her refuge, the place where she'd sought sanctuary when Richard had got his divorce. Until the divorce, they'd been living in a pretty semi-detached house in Chiswick, but even without its unhappy memories Olivia couldn't afford to keep it on. Instead, she'd moved into this rather gloomy apartment in Kensington and over the years she'd transformed its narrow rooms and draughty hallways into a place of light and beauty.

Henry came to meet her as she opened the door. Rubbing himself against her legs, he showed her how much he had missed her, but Olivia wasn't deceived. He was hungry, and he was reminding her it was his dinner time, and for the first time since she'd left Kay's office Olivia's generous lips curved in a smile.

'It's all right. I haven't forgotten you,' she said, juggling the two bags she'd brought from the supermarket and shouldering the door closed behind her. 'How does salmon and shrimp appeal to you?' Henry purred his approval as Olivia started down the hall. 'I should have known,' she added ruefully. 'It's only cupboard love.'

The kitchen smelled reassuringly of the plants and herbs she cultivated so assiduously. Trailing fronds of greenery brushed her face as she deposited the bags on the counter. There were daffodils on the window-ledge, providing a vivid splash of colour, and although the skies were overcast outside the kitchen was bright and cosily immune from the cold March wind.

Once Henry had been dealt with, Olivia filled the kettle and set it to boil. She would eat later, but for now she thought she deserved a hot, sweet cup of tea. As she put the food she'd bought away, she tried not to think of Diane Haran and her commission. This was her home; she didn't want to sully it with thoughts of her ex-husband's lover. She'd felt safe here, secure, far from the misery that loving Richard had brought.

With the tea made, she had no excuse for lingering in the kitchen, and, taking a deep breath, she pushed open the door to the office she'd created for herself. With the walls lined with books—both for pleasure and for reference—and a modern computer and printer, it was comfortingly familiar, her desk still as cluttered with papers as it had been when she went out.

Taking a sip of her tea, she perched on the old leather diplomat chair she'd bought at a warehouse sale three years ago, and regarded the clutter resignedly. She'd been planning on spending some time catching up with her correspondence, but there were still notes and discarded pages of manuscript from her last book lying around. That was why she'd been to see Kay that afternoon: to hear her judgement on her latest profile of a woman sailor. Suzanne Howard had sailed single-handedly around the world at the age of seventy-three.

The fact that Kay had been delighted by the manuscript had been eclipsed by the conversation they'd had about Diane Haran. But Olivia was relieved to know that what she was producing was still on track. When her first book— a biography of Catherine Parr, the only one of his six wives to have survived Henry the Eighth—had been successful, she'd been afraid it was only a one-off, that her next book would bomb as many second books did. But the life of Eileen Cusack had proved a best-seller, and that had encouraged her to approach the Howard family last year.

She wondered if Richard knew what she was doing. When he'd walked out, she'd been working for *Milady* magazine, with no prospect of improving her career. Perhaps if he hadn't walked out she wouldn't have found the nerve to tackle a book, she thought consideringly. It was true that he'd always made fun of the gossipy pieces she'd been paid to produce for the magazine.

Which brought her back to the subject she'd been trying to avoid ever since she'd left Kay's office. Was she actually going to write Diane Haran's story—or at least as much of it as the public would be permitted to know?

The shrilling of the telephone was a welcome escape from her thoughts, and, pushing back a strand of dark, toffee-coloured hair, she reached for the receiver. It crossed her mind, as she brought it to her ear, that it could be Kay, but it was too late now. Besides, she was fairly sure that Kay was satisfied that she'd promised to think about the commission. She was unlikely to try and push her any further. Not today, anyway.

'Yes?'

'Liv. At last!' It was her father. 'I've been trying to reach you all afternoon.' He paused, and when she didn't instantly jump in with an explanation he continued, 'Are you all right? Not having a problem with the new book, are you?'

'No.' Olivia blew out a breath. 'No, Kay's very happy with it, as it happens.' She forced herself to sound positive.

Her father and stepmother had supported her all through her divorce from Richard, and they'd be most disturbed to hear what she was thinking of doing. 'I—er—I was just at the supermarket. I've just got in.'

'Ah.' Matthew Pyatt sounded relieved. 'Well, your mother and I were wondering if you'd like to come for supper.' He always referred to her stepmother as her mother. After all, she had acted as such since Olivia was barely five years old. 'We've got something we want to discuss with you, and as we haven't seen you for a couple of weeks we thought it would kill two birds with one stone. What do you think?'

'Oh, Dad—' Olivia wasn't enthusiastic. After the afternoon she'd had, she'd been looking forward to doing nothing more energetic than putting a frozen pizza in the microwave and curling up with a bottle of wine. Besides, she needed time to think before Kay came back to her. And she wasn't sure she could hide her anxieties from them. 'Could I take a rain check?'

'There is something wrong.' Her father had always been incredibly perceptive, which was one of the reasons why she'd hoped to put him off. 'What is it? What's happened? You might as well tell me.'

Olivia sighed. 'Nothing's happened,' she said, not very convincingly, she had to admit. 'I'm—tired, that's all. It's been a stressful few weeks, finishing the book and—'

'Why are you stressed?' Her father broke in before she could warm to her theme. 'You're not being harassed by some man, are you? You read about these things in the papers—young women who live alone being terrorised in their homes. I've never been entirely happy with the security at the flat. Anyone can get in downstairs.'

'No, they can't.' Olivia was impatient. 'You know visitors have to use the intercom to get in.'

'But when that door opens to admit a legitimate visitor anyone can push in with them,' retorted her father. 'I know.

When I used to install heating systems, you'd be surprised at how many robberies there were.'

Olivia had to smile. 'I'm sure you don't mean that the way it sounded.'

'No, I don't.' Her father snorted. 'And you're not going to avoid an answer by being smug.'

'Oh, all right.' Olivia gave in. 'I'll come for supper.' She suppressed her misgivings. 'Just give me time to take a shower and change. Is eight o'clock all right?'

The Pyatts lived in Chiswick, just a stone's throw from the station. It gave Olivia quite a pang getting off the train at Grove Park station. For the four years that she and Richard had been married, she'd got off there every evening on her way home from work. But at least her father's house lay in the opposite direction to the one she used to take. The Pyatts' house was detached, with double gates and a block-paved drive leading to the front door.

Her stepmother opened the door to her.

'Liv, my dear.' Alice Pyatt reached up to bestow a warm kiss on her stepdaughter's cheek. 'Your father's just gone down to the cellar to get some wine. He'll be annoyed he wasn't here to greet you himself. He's been watching for you for the past half-hour.'

'Am I late?' Olivia let her stepmother help her off with her coat before stepping into the living room. There was a fire glowing in the hearth, and she moved towards it grate-fully. 'Mmm, this is cosy. I miss an open fire at the flat.'

Alice draped Olivia's overcoat over the banister and fol-lowed her stepdaughter into the room. 'You're not late,' she assured her. 'It's your father who's anxious. Now, what can I get you to drink? Sherry, perhaps, or a G and T?'

'Will I need one?' Olivia sank down into the armchair nearest the fire. 'You're looking well. Is that a new shade of lipstick you're wearing?'

'I am, and it is, but you're not going to get out of your father's questions that way,' responded Alice, with a smile.

'And I have to say you do look rather peaky. Something is wrong, isn't it? Your father's seldom mistaken.'

Olivia sighed. 'Nothing's wrong exactly,' she said, shaking her head at her stepmother's offer of the sherry she was pouring herself. 'I'll wait for the wine,' she added as Alice came to sit opposite her. And then, 'I don't look peaky, do I? I'm just feeling a bit—nervy, that's all.'

Alice shrugged and took a sip of her sherry, and, looking at the other woman, Olivia had to admit that she didn't look her age. As long as she could remember, Alice's hair had always been that particular shade of ash blonde, and although she knew it must be artificial now it still looked as soft and feminine as it had ever done.

'I'd say your father had some justification for his concern,' she declared now, crossing one silk-clad leg over the other.

Alice had good legs, too, and she'd never been afraid to display them to advantage. At fifty-five, she was ten years younger than her husband and looked at least twenty, and Olivia had always envied her plump, curvaceous figure.

'I've—I've been offered a new commission,' she said, deciding it might be easier to discuss it with her stepmother first. 'I'm just not sure whether I want to take it. It will mean living in the United States for a couple of months.'

'The United States!'

Alice sounded impressed, but before she could say anything more Matthew Pyatt strode into the room. 'The United States,' he echoed, bending to kiss his daughter. 'What about the United States? You're not going to live in New York, are you?'

'Of course not.' Olivia tried to breathe evenly, waiting until her father had lodged himself on the arm of his wife's chair before going on. 'It's just a—a commission I've been offered. In Los Angeles. I haven't decided whether I'm going to take it yet.'

'And that's what's on your mind, is it?' Matthew Pyatt stretched out his long legs towards the fire. His eyes narrowed. 'I must say, I'm not enthusiastic about you living out there either. A young woman, alone, in a volatile place like that.'

'I'm not a child, Dad.' Olivia wished she'd accepted a glass of sherry now. It would have given her something to do with her hands. As it was she clasped them between her legging-clad knees and pressed her legs together. 'It's not living in Los Angeles that's the problem.'

'Ah.' Her father nodded. 'You're concerned about us, is that it? Well—' he put an arm about his wife's shoulders '—that's what we wanted to talk to you about, actually. You know Alice has a sister living in New Zealand? As it happens, she's invited us to go out there for a couple of months, too. We were worried about leaving you alone, but if you're going to be away…'

Olivia swallowed. 'I see.'

'You don't mind, do you, Liv?' Alice leaned towards her anxiously, and Olivia knew she had to reassure them that that wasn't the case. But the truth was, she was a little apprehensive. It was as if all the circumstances were conspiring against her.

'I— Of course not,' she protested now, seeing the relief in her stepmother's face as she leaned back in her chair.

'That's good.' Alice smiled. 'It's nearly ten years since I saw Barbara.' She glanced up at her husband. 'That's one advantage of being retired. Matt won't be worrying about the business while we're gone.'

'So whose biography are you going to write now?' asked her father as his wife left the room to check on the supper, and Olivia knew she couldn't prevaricate any longer.

'Diane Haran's.' Her voice was flat. 'But I haven't decided yet whether I'm going to do it,' she added hastily as her father's face grew red. 'Don't look like that, Dad. It's a wonderful opportunity. And—and she and Richard are splitting up.'

'You're not serious!'

Matthew was on his feet now, and Olivia knew she had

been right to be apprehensive of seeking his advice. As far as her father was concerned, Richard Haig deserved a beating for the way he'd treated his daughter, and it was only because Olivia had pleaded with him not to get involved that they hadn't come to blows.

'Why not?' she asked, playing devil's advocate. 'According to Kay, I'll never be offered such a lucrative deal again.'

'You know why not,' grated her father. 'And that's why you're looking so worried, isn't it? I wondered why we hadn't seen you. I never suspected it was because of anything like this.'

'And it wasn't.' Olivia was indignant. 'Honestly, Dad, I just found out today. I've been doing the revisions on the other book. The one about Suzanne Howard. That's why I haven't seen you. Nothing else.'

Matthew Pyatt drew a steadying breath. 'But even so...'

'As I say, I haven't decided what I'm going to do yet,' said Olivia evenly, looping a strand of toffee-coloured hair behind her ear. Her hair was long, and she invariably wore it in a chignon when she was working, but this evening she'd created a rather precarious knot on top of her head.

Her father returned to the chair her stepmother had been occupying. 'But you are thinking of accepting it,' he pointed out. 'That's why you've mentioned it to me.'

'I've told you. I'm thinking about it.' Olivia half resented his interference. 'I'll let you know what I decide. It'll be before you leave for New Zealand, I expect.'

Her father scowled. 'I'm not sure I want to go to New Zealand now, knowing you're going to be seeing that swine again.' He sighed. 'Liv, there must be something else you can do. Can't you see, this woman's just using you to provide a convenient shoulder when she throws him out?'

That thought had occurred to Olivia, too, but she had no intention of admitting that to him. 'Let's leave it for now,' she begged. 'I'll let you know what I'm going to do.'

'And what about Henry?' Alice asked mischievously, after her husband had related Olivia's news to her, and Olivia thought how typical it was of her stepmother to try and lighten her husband's mood.

'Oh, my next-door neighbour will look after him,' said Olivia cheerfully. 'If I go, of course,' she added, with a nervous smile. 'But you're right, I can't forget the second most important man in my life.'

'And who's the first?' demanded her father grumpily.

'Why—you are, Daddy,' she assured him, meeting her stepmother's conspiratorial gaze.

CHAPTER TWO

DESPITE her decision, Olivia went through all the arguments why she shouldn't have accepted the commission on the flight from London to Los Angeles. At the very least, she knew her actions were open to all kinds of interpretation, and she preferred not to examine her motives too closely for fear of what she might find.

Her father wasn't pleased with her. And if he hadn't been going away himself she knew he'd have done everything in his power to persuade her not to do it. But, happily, Alice had been there to mediate for her, and they'd departed for Auckland on schedule just two weeks before her own flight was arranged.

And, on a purely objective level, she was quite excited at the prospect of spending several weeks in California. Although she'd been to New York before, she'd never travelled to the West Coast, and it was still sufficiently chilly in England to make the idea of a more temperate climate infinitely appealing.

The knowledge that she was probably going to see Richard again gave her mixed feelings. She couldn't deny that she was apprehensive, but she was also curious. She wanted to know what was happening in his life; whether the rumours about him and Diane were true. But most of all she wanted to know if she still cared about him. Whether her reasons for accepting this commission were as practical as she'd insisted.

She'd spent the month since she'd told Kay she would accept the commission researching Diane' s background in the East End of London, and she'd been surprised to learn how well thought of Diane still was amongst the people she'd grown up with. Contrary to the image Olivia had gained of a spoilt and selfish woman, the picture neighbours and classmates painted was of a generous, warm-hearted individual, who was not averse to helping out her friends in any way she could. Olivia was given dozens of anecdotes of the ways Diane had come through, from lending money when it was needed to offering her support when it was not.

According to the people Olivia had talked to, success had definitely not gone to Diane's head. She'd always been a little headstrong, they admitted, but she'd never forgotten her friends or her roots.

And her story was fascinating, Olivia had to admit. Fascinating, amazing, harrowing, at times, but always interesting. The eldest of a family of seven children—many of them with different fathers—her childhood had been blighted by poverty and abuse. Her mother, who had been described as both hard-working and ignorant, had had little time for any of her children, and Diane, as the eldest, had been expected to help care for her younger siblings.

From the beginning, Diane's outstanding physical beauty had caused problems and she'd become sexually aware at a very young age. But, ironically enough, it was because of an older man's attraction to the fifteen-year-old Diane that she'd become famous. A wealthy man, he'd taken her to dine at a swish London restaurant and she'd caught the eye of a fashion photographer who was looking for a face for the 'eighties'.

The rest was history, as they say, but Olivia guessed there was more to it than that. The years between could not have been easy, and although she was loath to admit it Olivia couldn't help seeing her subject in a different light.

Which was just as well for the job she had to do, she acknowledged. This biography had to be objective, and she was glad that the research she'd already done had enabled her to amend her opinion. Why Diane should have wanted her to write her story was something she had yet to find out. Perhaps she really had enjoyed Eileen Cusack's biography, Olivia reflected ruefully. After the things she'd learned, anything was possible.

But not probable, the small voice inside her argued as the big jet banked to make its approach to LAX. The sprawling mass that was Los Angeles was spread out below her, and there was no turning back. She was here; she was committed; and she had to stop worrying about Richard and concentrate on the job.

The oval-shaped airport buildings gleamed in the afternoon sunlight as the plane taxied along the runway. It was incredible to think that they'd left London at lunchtime and yet it was still only a quarter to four here. The miracle of international time zones, she thought as the aircraft approached its landing bay. She'd worry about the jet lag later.

The passengers were transferred from the plane to an air-conditioned walkway that conducted them to Passport Control. Because the expenses she was being allowed had enabled her to sit in the Club World section of the British Airways jet, Olivia found herself among the first to reach the Arrivals Hall, and like everyone else she spent the time waiting for her luggage by people-spotting.

She recognised a couple of famous faces who had apparently been travelling in the first-class compartment of the plane, and was surprised at the lack of interest shown towards them. It wasn't until she noticed the bodyguards, tucked discreetly behind a pillar, that she understood her mistake. But still, it was something to tell her parents when she got home.

She had been checking that her luggage tags were still safely attached to her boarding pass when she looked up to find a man watching her. The fact that his clothes looked expensive and he was wearing a Rolex watch should have reassured her, but it didn't. It just reminded her of how vulnerable she was as a stranger here.

Diane's secretary had faxed her that she would meet her at the airport, and she hoped she kept her word. Still, she could always take a taxi, she assured herself impatiently. She knew Diane's address and she wasn't a child.

Indeed, she thought ruefully, her height would be a deterrent for most men. And although she was slim she knew she was fairly strong. She wasn't a fitness freak, but she did enjoy swimming and cycling, and she knew from her experiences in New York that in the normal way she had nothing to be afraid of.

Unless her imaginary attacker looked like the man who had been watching her, she conceded, relieved to see that he had apparently lost interest. He was staring towards the carousel that would eventually spill out their luggage, and she found herself observing him with rather more interest than sense.

He was certainly big, she mused, and dark, with a lean, sinewy grace that was nothing like the muscle-bound heroes Hollywood seemed to spawn with such regularity. And although he was good to look at his appeal lay in the roughness of his features rather than their uniformity. Deep-set eyes beneath dark brows, and narrow cheekbones and a thin-lipped mouth; if there were lines on his face, they were lines of experience, and she realised he was probably ten years older than the twenty-five she'd originally judged him to be.

She wondered who he was. Not a film star, she decided, though there was another man hovering close by who could be a minder. If he needed one, she speculated doubtfully, realising she was being far too nosy. Whoever he was, he wasn't interested in her, and she was unlikely to see him again.

The carousel had begun to turn and suitcases appeared like magic from the chute above it. A black holdall appeared, and the man standing beside the man she had been watching went to rescue it. She noticed he also had a suit carrier looped across his shoulder, and after he'd plucked the holdall from the conveyor he and his companion turned towards the exit.

First class, Olivia informed herself silently, realising the two men must have travelled on the same flight from London. She grimaced. So what? It was nothing to do with her. It was time she started paying attention to her own luggage. She thought she could see one of her suitcases just starting along the metal belt.

'Would you happen to be Ms Pyatt?'

The unfamiliar voice was amazingly sexy. It conjured up images of hot sultry nights and bare brown limbs tangled in satin sheets. Olivia decided she was in danger of acting out her own fantasies, and, blaming the man who had fired her imagination, she turned to find that he hadn't left after all but was standing right behind her.

'I—' Swallowing to ease the dryness of her throat, she started over. 'Yes,' she said, a little reluctantly. 'I'm Olivia Pyatt.' She'd reverted to her own surname when she and Richard were divorced. Then, because it was the only thing she could think of, she asked, 'Did Miss Haran ask you to meet me?'

The man's lean mouth twitched. 'Not exactly,' he said, humour tugging at the corners of his lips. 'But Diane told me you were travelling on this flight.'

So he did know Diane. Olivia breathed a little more easily, although common sense told her it was the only explanation. 'Did you travel from London, too?' she asked, as if she didn't already know that he had. He was probably a Californian, which would explain his accent and his tan.

'Yeah.' He glanced towards his companion, who was waiting patiently for him to finish. 'B.J. and I make the trip fairly regularly.' He grimaced. 'It's not to be recommended.'

'Because of the jet lag?' guessed Olivia, aware that her suitcase was about to start going round again. 'Excuse me, I must get my luggage. I don't want to have to carry it any further than I have to.'

'I'll get it.'

Leaning past her, the man lifted the heavy bag off the carousel and set it down beside her. In jeans and a light cotton jacket, he moved much easier than she did in her corduroy suit. The suit had seemed reasonably lightweight, too, when she'd left London, but she was already sweating.

But that could be because of the present situation, she conceded. She wasn't used to being accosted by strange men.

'Is this all?' he asked, and for a moment she didn't know what he was talking about. 'Your luggage,' he prompted, and, glancing up at him, she noticed he had tawny eyes. Like a cat, she thought, realising she was behaving stupidly. For God's sake, he was being polite. Nothing else.

'Um—no, there's one more,' she said hurriedly, scanning the conveyor. 'It's always the way, isn't it? One comes, and then you've got to wait for ever for the other.' She glanced towards his companion, who was still standing with the holdall in his hand and the suit carrier draped over his shoulder. 'Please—don't let me keep you. I'm sure your friend must be getting impatient.'

'B.J.?' He, too, glanced the other man's way, and then turned back to give Olivia a lazy smile. 'No sweat,' he said as Olivia's toes curled inside her Doc Martens. 'It's cooler in here than outside.'

'Oh, but—' Olivia wanted to ask why he was waiting with her, but she couldn't. Loosening the tight cuffs of her jacket, she peeled them back over her wrists. 'Um—do you think Miss Haran's secretary will be waiting outside? She said she'd come to meet me herself.'

'Bonnie?'

He had the name right, and Olivia nodded. 'A Miss Lovelace,' she agreed, not used to using the woman's given name.

'I guess she'll be waiting in the Arrivals Hall,' he responded carelessly. 'I'll point her out to you when we go through.'

Olivia caught her lower lip between her teeth. 'I—gather you're a friend of Miss Haran's,' she said awkwardly, and he made a husky sound of disbelief.

'Hell, yes,' he said. 'I'm sorry; I didn't introduce myself, did I? I'm Joe Castellano. I—guess you could say I have an investment in Diane's career.'

He held out his hand, and Olivia had no choice but to shake it, hoping he wouldn't be too put off by her sweaty palm. 'How do you do, Mr Castellano?' she said, wondering if he was a frequent visitor to Diane's Beverly Hills mansion. It would be rather nice, she thought, if he was.

She barely had time to extract her hand before she saw her other suitcase approaching. There were quite a lot of people gathered round the carousel now, and she saw several of the women weighing up the man at her side. And why not? she thought ruefully. He was attractive. Was he married? she wondered, rather foolishly. He was wearing a signet ring on his right hand but that was all.

When her suitcase was within reach, she lunged for it, staggering as the unexpected weight of the bag pulled at her arm. 'Let me,' he said shortly, and she felt his impatience. He set the suitcase down and summoned a porter with a trolley. 'I guess we can get moving now?'

'Right.'

She had little choice but to follow the porter, and to her relief they passed through the Customs channel without incident. It crossed her mind as they were walking past the officials that he could be a drug smuggler using her as cover. But she decided she was allowing her imagination to get the better of her again. Just because he had an Italian surname, that did not mean he was connected to the 'mob'.

Beyond the baggage collection area, a barrier separated arriving passengers from those waiting to meet them, and Olivia immediately saw her name on a board being held up by a woman at the end of a line of similar boards.

'That must be Miss Lovelace,' she said to her companion, nodding towards the rather harassed-looking woman with tinted blonde hair and immaculate make-up who was scanning the new arrivals. Olivia guessed the woman was in her forties but her skirt was shorter than anything she'd have worn herself.

He nodded. 'Yeah, that's Bonnie. But don't call her Miss Lovelace. She prefers the anonymous *Ms.*' He grinned at Olivia, and once again she was struck by his magnetism. 'You're going to be dealing with some tender egos here. Keep that in mind.'

The woman had seen them now but from her expression Olivia guessed she hadn't made any connection between them. Or perhaps she had and it was the wrong one, she reflected doubtfully. It was flattering to think Miss Lovelace—*Ms* Lovelace, she corrected herself firmly—had assumed she was travelling with him. But this was the moment when she had to come down to earth.

'Hey, Joe.' Bonnie Lovelace greeted him like a long-lost friend. Then her eyes moved suspiciously to Olivia. 'Diane said you'd be on this flight. She's missed you. Did you have a good trip?'

'The usual,' drawled Joe as the porter halted uncertainly beside them. He slipped a note into the man's hand and indicated Olivia. 'These ladies will show you where their transport is parked.'

Bonnie Lovelace's jaw dropped as she turned back to Olivia. 'You're Ms Pyatt?' she exclaimed, and Joe touched her shoulder with a mocking hand.

'Who else?' he asked. 'I just thought I'd do my good deed for the day and deliver her into your hands, Bonnie.' He arched a brow at Olivia. 'Take care. I'm sure I'll see you around.'

Olivia didn't know who was the most deflated as he strolled off with the man he'd called B.J. but she suspected it had to be her, judging by the way she felt. She swallowed her chagrin. So—he was a friend of Diane's. She'd been told as much so why did she feel so disappointed now?

'Ms Pyatt.' Bonnie seemed to come to her senses, too, and, holding out her hand, she took Olivia's in a limp grip. 'You must forgive me,' she said. 'I didn't realise it was you with Joe—er—with Mr Castellano.' She gestured to the porter to follow them and as they moved along she added, 'Did you travel out together? How did he know who you were?'

'He—helped me with my luggage so I suppose he read the labels,' said Olivia after a moment, curiously loath to discuss the details of how they'd met. It was nothing to do with this woman after all. She was just curious. Probably wondering why he'd even bothered to speak to her, she thought glumly, changing her tote bag from one shoulder to the other.

'Mmm.' Bonnie gave her another assessing look, and then excused herself to head first through the glass doors that gave onto the concourse outside. 'I left Manuel in the car,' she added, glancing about her as the porter halted beside them. 'Oh, there he is.' She waved her arm at a man seated behind the wheel of a huge Mercedes. 'It's so difficult to find a parking space. Do you have this problem back home?'

'Sometimes,' answered Olivia absently, her attention caught by the sleek black saloon that was just moving past them. Joe Castellano was at the wheel, and he raised one hand in a casual salute. 'Um—' She gathered her wits. 'I don't own a car, actually. It's not worth it in London, and if I want to go further I have an old Harley-Davidson in the garage.'

Bonnie stopped in the act of lifting the boot lid of the Mercedes to stare at her. 'You ride a motorcycle?' she exclaimed in horror. And then said, 'Well, I guess you are tall enough at that.'

'Yeah, right.' Olivia weathered the back-handed compliment with her usual forbearance, and as Manuel slid out from behind the wheel to open the rear door for her she slipped inside.

Soft leather, air-conditioning and the fragrance of expensive perfume were some consolation. Unbelievable, she thought, stretching her long legs luxuriously. Wait until she could tell her stepmother about this! Unlike her father, Alice had been able to see the advantages of what she was being offered, and there was no doubt that it was going to be an experience she wouldn't forget.

Which reminded her that she hadn't thought of her ex-husband for the past half hour. From the moment Joe Castellano had spoken to her, she'd completely forgotten that she'd soon be seeing Richard again. Oh, God, she thought as the realisation that she was actually here in

California penetrated the haze of anticipation she was feeling. She dreaded to think what his reaction was going to be.

Bonnie got in beside her at that moment, which prevented her from continuing along that stony track. And besides, she chided herself, she shouldn't care what Richard might think. It was Diane who had invited her. If he had any complaints he should take them up with her.

She expelled a deep breath and turned to look out of the window. She realised that for the first time since she'd been offered this commission she was actually feeling optimistic about the result. It was foolish, probably—*definitely*—but somehow meeting Joe Castellano had given a boost to her confidence. Richard wasn't the only man in the world. She'd been nursing her broken heart for far too long.

'There we are.' Bonnie seated herself beside her and cast the younger woman a relieved look. 'This place gets more and more like a bull ring. I swear to God I'll have a heart attack if I have to fight my way out of here one more time!'

'I'm sorry.' Olivia felt responsible. She watched Manuel get back behind the wheel and start the engine. 'Anyway, thank you for coming to meet me. I could have got a taxi, I suppose—'

'Diane wouldn't hear of it.' Bonnie interrupted her to make her point. 'So—you had a good flight, yeah? What was the movie? These days, the only time I get to see a decent movie is on a plane.'

'Oh, well, I'm afraid I didn't—' began Olivia, only to find her companion wasn't listening.

'Yeah, movies,' Bonnie went on reminiscently. 'You'd think living in a town like this I'd be up on all the latest blockbusters. But, you know what? I spend all my time watching television instead.'

'Really?' said Olivia. 'I like television, too.' Or she had since the break-up of her marriage. Somehow, she couldn't see herself as part of the singles scene again.

''Cause working for Diane takes up most of my day, so when I get home I'm exhausted,' Bonnie continued, almost

as if Olivia hadn't spoken. She flapped an expansive hand.
'I guess you'll get used to it. I swear to God, I sometimes
think Diane's too generous for her own good.'

Olivia nodded now, but she didn't make the mistake of
trying to join in again, and she saw Manuel watching her
with an amused expression on his olive-skinned face. He
winked at her in the rear-view mirror, and she hid a smile.
Obviously he was used to Ms Lovelace. Perhaps Olivia
should call her *Miss*. That might get her attention.

But she decided against it. It was too nice a day to spoil
it, and the last thing she wanted to do was make an enemy
here. She had yet to discover what Diane's attitude towards
her was going to be, and until she did it was safer to play
it cool.

Beyond the car's tinted windows, the streets of the City
of the Angels shimmered in the late afternoon sun. Olivia
was looking forward to the prospect of taking a shower and
changing into something cooler. She hoped she'd have time
to freshen up before she met her hostess. She wondered
where she was going to stay. Kay had merely said that
Diane's secretary had made the arrangements. Perhaps
she'd be expected to stay at the house. Again, according to
Kay, Diane's mansion was quite a showplace.

Their route from the airport was not immediately inspiring, however. They passed what seemed like dozens of car
dealerships and abandoned warehouses, with strip malls il-
luminated with garish neon signs. She saw houses with
flaking porches, and incongruously customised vehicles in
hot metallic shades. It made it easier for her to grasp the
fact that she was actually here. She'd read somewhere that
Los Angeles had taken over from Ellis Island as the most
heavily burdened immigration point in the United States.

They drove north through sprawling suburbs, passing
signs for well-known districts like Marina del Rey and
Santa Monica. Olivia seemed to remember there was a pier
at Santa Monica, and she guessed there was surfing, too.
She couldn't quite see herself standing up on a surfboard,

she mused, deliberately avoiding thoughts of her destination and what it would mean.

Santa Monica Boulevard drove through the heart of the wealthiest district of Los Angeles. Olivia recognised the names of some of the hotels they passed, and Bonnie pointed out the 'HOLLYWOOD' sign that towered over what had once been the movie capital of the world. Nowadays, the glitz had become rather tarnished, she told Olivia laconically. But there was still a thriving film community, supplemented by the successful soap stars from TV.

Beverly Hills lay to the west of Hollywood, but to Olivia's surprise they turned off before the road wound up into the quiet streets far away from the commercial district. A couple of turns and they were in Hunter Plaza, with the Moorish arches of the Beverly Plaza Hotel fronting its famous façade.

Olivia was still admiring the square-cut towers that rose behind its entrance when Manuel drove into the courtyard and stopped before the double glass doors. A major domo stepped forward instantly and opened the door of the limousine, and Bonnie said, 'Welcome to America,' before stepping out and gesturing to Olivia to do the same. 'I'm sure you're going to be very comfortable here.'

'Here' turned out to be a penthouse suite situated on the top floor of the twelve-storey hotel. While Manuel handed her bags over to one of the hotel's bellboys, Bonnie checked her in, and Olivia realised that it was only a formality by the speed with which Bonnie was given her key. Well, not a key, exactly, she learned, when Bonnie demonstrated how to use the laminated card. Apparently, the code was changed every time a new resident took possession of the room, the card being pressed into the slot to open the door of the suite. The card was obviously easier and lighter to carry around, too.

The suite itself was the most luxurious apartment Olivia could have imagined. Airy, high-ceilinged, furnished in delicate shades of green and blue, with expansive views of

Beverly Hills and the hazy downtown areas, it was apparently where she was going to stay. 'You're sort of in back of the Beverly Wiltshire,' explained Bonnie, mentioning the name of one of the landmark hotels. 'That's Rodeo Drive down there.'

Olivia guessed she was supposed to be impressed, but in fact she was feeling a bit let down. However reluctant she might have been to meet Diane—and possibly Richard—she'd been ready for it. Now she felt deflated, aware that at some future time she was going to have to face it again.

'You like it, don't you?' Bonnie was looking a little worried now and Olivia guessed that however indifferent the woman might be to her feelings she was anxious that Diane should have nothing to complain about. 'See.' She opened another door. 'This is the bedroom. And that's the bath— you've got a spa bath and a Jacuzzi—through there.'

'Very nice.'

Olivia tried to sound enthusiastic, but it wasn't easy. However luxurious it might be, it wasn't home. She half wished she'd insisted on making her own arrangements for accommodation. A small hotel would have suited her better than this.

'The hotel can supply you with a PC,' added Bonnie briskly. 'Diane didn't know what you'd need so she's left that up to me. I'll be checking in with you all the time, so that's not a problem, and Diane was sure that you'd work more easily here.'

And keep out of her hair.

The words were unspoken, but as the bellboy came in with her luggage and Bonnie went to tip him Olivia gazed around the suite with a cynical eye. Was this what Richard had really abandoned her for? she wondered. This wealthy lifestyle? What price now his accusations that she couldn't give him the children he wanted? As far as she knew, he and Diane hadn't had any children either. Though, of course, that could be her decision, not his.

'D'you need any help with your unpacking?'

The bellboy had departed now and Bonnie was regarding

her with a vaguely irritated air. Olivia guessed her reaction hadn't been the one she'd expected. She wondered if the secretary knew that Richard had once been married to her. Somehow, she doubted it.

'No,' she answered now, slipping off her corduroy jacket. It was quite a relief to feel the air-conditioned air cooling her bare arms. 'Um—thank you,' she added, almost as an afterthought. 'I can manage, really. You've been very kind.'

'Well, good.' Bonnie was mollified by her reply and with a tight smile she gave the apartment another thorough look. 'I suggest you rest up for a while, and then order yourself some dinner from Room Service. You'll have plenty of time to explore the hotel when your body's caught up with your mind.'

Olivia nodded. It was true: she was feeling a little dazed, and it wasn't just the shock of her arrival at the hotel. Perhaps Diane was right; perhaps she would be glad to have a place of her own to return to. Once she got used to it, that was. Right now, she was too exhausted to care.

CHAPTER THREE

IN FACT, Olivia left most of her unpacking until the next morning. After Bonnie left, she felt too exhausted to do much more than take out her nightshirt and the bag containing her toothbrush and soap. A shower, in a fluted glass cubicle, refreshed her sufficiently to order a light supper, but she fell asleep without finishing the shrimps and salad they'd brought her.

She was awake before it was light. Her watch said it was lunchtime, but the clock on the bedside cabinet told a different story. Four o'clock! she thought, in dismay. At least three hours until she could order an early breakfast. Goodness, how long would it take her body to adjust to an eight-hour time change? She'd be falling asleep when by Pacific time it would only be four p.m.

She was hungry now, so she rescued one of the bread rolls they'd supplied her with the night before and spread it with butter. The coffee was cold, but the water from the tap was a palatable alternative, and after enjoying her small feast she fell asleep again.

The next time she opened her eyes, a pale dawn was turning the sky to palest yellow, with fluffy white clouds shredding before the rising sun. Slipping off the huge bed, she went somewhat disbelievingly to the window. She was actually here, in California, she thought, running a hand through the tumbled weight of her hair. Incredible! Twenty-four hours ago she had just been leaving London.

She discovered, when she rang down for breakfast, that it was in fact a twenty-four-hour room service, which meant she could have ordered herself a snack at four a.m. Still, it was much more pleasant to eat cereal with fresh strawberries and scrambled eggs seated at the table in the window with the sunshine streaming over her. She felt much brighter this morning, and far more optimistic than she'd done the night before.

She'd unpacked her suitcases while she'd been waiting for her breakfast, and in consequence she was dressed and ready by eight o'clock. She'd taken another shower and decided on a simple short-skirted dress of lime-green cotton, and because her hair was too silky from the shampoo to behave neatly she'd used a scarf to hold it back instead.

The effect was quite dramatic for her, and she studied her reflection for some time before turning away. Was her skirt too short? Was her neckline too low? Should she have chosen something more businesslike? She realised she was starting to spook herself, and dismissed her misgivings. She'd need all the ammunition she possessed to face the interview ahead.

Assuming that no one was likely to contact her before nine o'clock, Olivia decided to go and take a look at the rest of the hotel. She knew that if she stayed in the suite she'd start worrying, and it would be much better if she kept her mind occupied with something other than the reason why she was here. Besides, she told herself fiercely, she was curious about her surroundings, and if she was staying here for any length of time she should know where everything was.

The lift transported her down to the foyer without incident, and she discovered that far from being the only person who was up and about the ground floor of the hotel was fairly buzzing with activity. She remembered now that when she'd stayed in New York she'd noticed this same phenomenon. Americans very often held business meetings at breakfast, and as if to prove this there were lots of immaculately suited men and women with briefcases passing in and out of the terrace restaurant.

They reminded her of Joe Castellano, and she wondered if he ever ate breakfast at this hotel. It was an unlikely scenario, she had to admit. Did she actually think he might come looking for her?

Brushing such a ridiculous thought aside, she saw the

glint of a swimming pool through the long windows that
flanked a palm-shaded courtyard. The hotel appeared to be
built around this inner courtyard, and she moved towards
the automatic doors that gave access to the pool area.
Striped umbrellas, cushioned loungers and a wealth of thick
towels piled on an old-fashioned handcart invited investi-
gation. The whole place had a 'twenties' feel about it, but
the facilities were as luxurious as they come.

Still, it was good to know that she could take a swim
whenever she felt like it. She could imagine how delightful
that would be in the heat of the day. She smiled. She was
in danger of enjoying this temporary exile. She had to remember exactly why she was here.

She'd had no problem remembering last night. Then, the
strangeness of her surroundings, the fact that she hadn't met
Diane, after all, and the news that she was to stay here and
not at her subject's mansion, had left her feeling decidedly
down. The only bright spot in her day had been her meeting
with Joe Castellano at the airport, but she was intelligent
enough to know that she was unlikely ever to run into him
again.

But he had been kind, and because of him she hadn't
done anything stupid. Like trying to ring Richard, or crying
herself to sleep. And this morning she could safely say she
was looking forward to starting work. That was the only
reason she was here, she assured herself. She didn't care if
she saw Richard or not.

She sighed. As she sauntered round the huge pool, she
was forced to acknowledge that her last assertion wasn't
precisely true. She did want to see Richard again—but only
to reassure herself that he was all right, she told herself
firmly. They had known one another for a long time, after
all. It was natural that she should care what happened to
him.

The fact that he hadn't particularly cared what happened
to her when he walked out on her followed on from this
assumption. But she wasn't like Richard, she reminded herself. She did care about people's feelings. She couldn't help

it. But what she had to remember was that Richard had hurt
her. She mustn't give him the chance to hurt her all over
again.

The message light was flashing on the phone when she
got back to her suite. Checking in with the receptionist, she
learned that a car was coming to pick her up at ten o'clock.
She was asked to be waiting in the foyer at that time, and
she guessed that Bonnie Lovelace would be coming along
to identify her to the driver.

Which left her just a short time to worry about her appearance. Having seen so much informal attire downstairs,
she wondered if she ought to wear shorts. But no. Meeting
Diane again, she wanted to look half decent. And a vest
and shorts would put their association on far too familiar a
level.

She was downstairs at five to ten, still wearing the lime-
green cotton, with a tote bag containing her notebook and
tape recorder slung over her shoulder. She'd managed to
tame her hair into a French braid so it looked considerably
tidier, and she'd added a pair of gold earloops for good
measure.

'Liv?'

She'd been watching the antics of a toddler, who'd got
away from his mother and was presently causing a lot of
grief to one of the waiters who was trying to serve coffee
from the foyer bar, when a hand touched her shoulder. She
hadn't been aware of anyone's approach, and the unexpected British accent took her by surprise. She swung
round, all thoughts of hiding her feelings going out of her
head, and stared at the man behind her with her heart in
her eyes.

'Richard!'

'Hello, Liv.'

His response was every bit as emotional as hers had been
and before she knew what he was doing he'd bent his head
and bestowed a lingering kiss on her mouth. His lips were
warm and wet, as if he'd been licking them in anticipation,
and although Olivia had expected to be gratified by the

warmth of his greeting she found she didn't care for his assumption that she'd welcome it.

'I've missed you so much, Liv,' he added, and she was dismayed to see that his eyes had filled with tears. Eyes that were slightly red-rimmed, she noticed, with a telling puffiness beneath each one.

Indeed, as she came to look at him properly, she saw that his eyes weren't the only evidence of change about him. He'd put on weight, for one thing. His limbs had thickened, and his stomach swelled over the leather of his belt. He'd bleached his hair, too, and although it accentuated his tan it looked artificial. In a polo shirt and shorts, he looked little like the man she remembered.

'You look—terrific,' he went on, surveying her slim figure and bare legs with greedy eyes. 'Come on.' He gestured towards the exit. 'I've got the car waiting.' His lips twisted. 'Is Diane going to get a shock when she sees you!'

'I doubt it.'

Olivia let him escort her towards the glass doors with some reluctance. Although it was true that she had lost weight since the divorce, otherwise she looked much the same. Her hair was longer, of course. When she'd been married to Richard and working in the city, it had been easier to handle when it was shorter. But compared to Diane Haran—or should she say Diane *Haig*?—she was very ordinary indeed.

And no one knew that better than Richard himself.

Outside, the limousine in which she and Bonnie had travelled from the airport the previous afternoon was waiting, with Manuel at the wheel. Actually, Olivia was quite relieved to see the chauffeur. For a moment, she'd wondered if Richard had come alone. But, whether the unhappy rumours about his marriage were true or not, Diane had evidently decided they needed a chaperon. Or perhaps it was the fact that, even at this early hour of the morning, Olivia could smell the sour scent of alcohol on Richard's breath.

Once they were in the car, she took care to put a good twelve inches of white leather between them, and Richard turned to give her a wounded look. 'Don't you trust me, Liv?' he protested, making an abortive attempt to take her hand. 'God, you didn't used to look at me like that. What an unholy mess I've made of both our lives.'

Olivia caught her breath at this assertion. Although he was staring straight ahead, she prayed Manuel wasn't listening to Richard's maudlin complaints. Not only was he full of self-pity, but he was acting as if she shared his regrets.

And she didn't.

Well, not really, she amended, trying to be brutally honest with herself. She couldn't deny that she'd hoped it hadn't been all plain sailing for him. She was human, after all, and when Kay had said his marriage to Diane was in trouble she had felt a quiver of anticipation. But she'd never expected that Richard might really want to see her. Or that he might covet what he'd lost.

'So—how are you?' Richard asked now, evidently deciding he'd said enough about his feelings for the present.

'I'm fine,' she answered, with determined brightness. 'The jet lag's a bit of a problem. I was awake at four o'clock; can you believe that?' She grimaced. 'Thank goodness I managed to go back to sleep.'

Richard relaxed against the soft upholstery, one arm spread expansively along the back of the seat. 'It affects different people in different ways,' he said carelessly. 'Myself, it's no problem. But then, I'm used to travelling a lot.'

Olivia wound the strap of her bag round her fingers. 'With Diane?' she asked, and he gave her a jaded look.

'I used to,' he said. 'I used to think she wanted me with her. But these days I usually stay at home.'

Olivia pressed her lips together. 'Well, you certainly have a beautiful place to live in,' she murmured, gazing out of the car window. She didn't know what to say, what to think, and it was easier to talk about impersonal things. 'Is this Beverly Hills?' she asked as the limousine wound its way up quiet streets flanked by high hedges and stone walls. There was little to see of the estates that sprawled behind the wrought-iron security gates.

'You've been in Beverly Hills since you left the hotel,' replied Richard indifferently. 'This whole area is known as the City of Beverly Hills. What a laugh! It's really just the west side of Los Angeles. But people like my wife think it's paradise on earth.'

'Oh, I'm sure—'

'She does. I'm telling you. Diane's really into this West Coast lifestyle. My God, I don't think a scrap of meat has passed her lips in the last four years! It's all fruit and cereal and therapy and body massage. God, you don't know how sick of it all I am, Liv. That's why I'm so glad to have you here.'

'Richard—'

'It's not real, Liv. The people who live here don't live in the real world any more.' He cast a disparaging glance out of the window at the walled estates. 'Fortress America! Can you honestly say you know what all the excitement is about?'

Olivia's lower lip curled between her teeth and she bit on it, hard. It seemed obvious that whatever comment she made Richard was going to put it down. When had he got so cynical? she wondered unhappily. She didn't know what to say so she decided to hold her tongue.

'I suppose I should congratulate you on your success,' he remarked, after a moment, and once again she heard the bitterness in his voice. 'My Liv, an author! Who'd have thought it? I told you you were wasted at that rag you used to work for.'

He hadn't, actually. Quite the reverse, but she didn't contradict him. She had no desire to arrive at Diane's estate while he was in this mood. If she wasn't careful he'd be crying on her shoulder. God knew what Diane would say if she found out.

She wished he'd pull himself together and stop treating her like an accomplice. As if the only reason she'd come here was to be with him. She drew an uneven breath. She was beginning to wonder what she'd ever seen in him. Had he always blamed other people when things went wrong?

The memory of what he'd said when they'd been trying to have a family returned to haunt her. Although they'd both had tests and there'd seemed no reason why they shouldn't have a baby, she knew he'd blamed her. And perhaps it was her fault, she reflected. They'd probably never know. And at that time she'd been far more willing to blame herself.

'I meant what I said, you know, Liv,' he muttered, attracting her attention. 'I have missed you more than you'll ever know. Leaving you was the biggest mistake I've ever made in my life. I wanted to tell you that right from the start.'

'Then you shouldn't have!' exclaimed Olivia hotly, convinced that Manuel could hear what he was saying. He had no right to involve her in his marital problems, whatever excuse he thought he had. She chewed her lip. She suspected his confession was a deliberate attempt to gain her sympathy, and also make her a party to his resentment whether she liked it or not.

'I can't help myself,' he told her now, and once again she had to suffer his efforts to touch her. His arm along the back of the seat descended onto her shoulders and she felt his fingers stroking her neck. 'I know I hurt you, Liv, but I'm hoping you'll find it in your heart to forgive me. The love we shared—I can't believe we let it go.'

'*You* let it go, Richard,' said Olivia flatly, removing his arm from her shoulder and shifting onto the opposite seat. She glanced about her. 'Is it much further?'

Richard heaved a heavy sigh. 'No,' he said, and although his tone was sulky Olivia was relieved. Sulky was acceptable; tearful wasn't. She gave a slight shake of her head. She couldn't believe this was happening to her.

The limousine began to slow a few minutes later, and as Olivia glanced round to see where they were Manuel turned between wrought-iron gates that had opened at their approach. A long curving drive confronted them, hedged with laurel and acacia, and she felt her nerves tighten as they drove up to the house.

A pillared façade of cream sandstone confronted them. Within its shadows, a shaded loggia stretched along the front of the house. Built on two floors, its many windows protected by terracotta-painted shutters, it was large and impressive, with a wealth of flowering shrubs and trees surrounding its manicured lawns.

'Well, this is it,' said Richard sardonically as Manuel got out of his seat to open the rear doors. 'The Villa Mariposa. Are you ready to meet your employer?'

'She's not my employer,' said Olivia, rather too vehemently, and was annoyed when Richard's lips curved in a knowing smile.

'No, she's not,' he applauded, 'and don't you let her forget it.' He clutched her arm, and she was forced to follow him out of the car. 'Go for it, Liv,' he added softly. 'I knew you weren't as indifferent to me as you pretended.'

Olivia dragged her arm away as soon as she was able, aware that once again Manuel was watching their exchange with curious eyes. And who could blame him? she thought, regarding Richard with some frustration. This was hard enough without Richard making it worse.

The doors at the top of the shallow flight of steps had opened, and Olivia glanced somewhat apprehensively in that direction. But she saw to her relief that it was just a maid who stood there, dressed in a navy uniform and a white apron.

She gestured for Olivia to come up the steps and offered a polite smile as they entered a cool marble-floored reception hall with an arched ceiling stretching up two floors. At its peak, a circular stained-glass window cast a rainbow shaft of sunlight down into the hall, while the gentle hum of air-conditioning prevented any surge of heat.

'Mees Haran is waiting by the pool, Mees Pyatt,' she said, inviting Olivia to follow her. And her announcement solved Olivia's other problem of what to call Richard's wife.

'Thank you.'

Olivia shouldered her tote bag, and, not caring whether Richard was following them or not, she accompanied the maid across the hall. An arched doorway exposed several steps down into a sunlit garden room, where a pair of glass doors stood wide to a flagged terrace. Rattan tables and chairs stood in the shade of the upstairs balcony, and a pair of inquisitive sparrows picked crumbs from between the stones.

There were flowers everywhere, Olivia noticed. In pots and planters in the garden room, in tubs and hanging baskets on the terrace, and climbing over the columns that supported the balcony above. The scent was glorious, but perhaps a little overpowering, and she was glad when they descended more steps and she glimpsed the aquamarine waters of the pool glinting below them.

She saw Diane at once.

The woman she had never expected to meet again was propped on a cushioned lounge chair, with a huge yellow umbrella protecting her from the direct rays of the sun. Although she must have known that Olivia had arrived, she didn't look in her direction. Her attention was focussed on a child who was splashing about at the edge of the pool beside her.

Her child?

Olivia caught her breath. If it was, it had been a well-kept secret. She couldn't believe she wouldn't have heard about Diane's having a child if it had appeared in the press. Richard's child, too? she wondered, aware of a not unnatural sense of envy. Not for the fact that it was Richard's child, she assured herself, but because she would have so much liked a child of her own.

Diane had evidently heard the sound of her feet on the tiled apron, and with another quick word to her companion she got smoothly to her feet. In a one-piece bathing suit with exotic orchids adorning its navy background, she looked magnificent. No sign of excess flesh here, thought

Olivia ruefully. Diane was every bit as beautiful as she recalled.

'Hi,' Diane said, by way of a greeting, coming to meet her. Her bare feet left damp patches on the tiles, revealing that she had been in the water, too. It made her seem more human, somehow, Olivia thought, aware of how tense she was feeling. No statue, this, but a living, breathing woman.

'Hello.'

The word stuck in Olivia's throat, making any further speech impossible at that moment, and she glanced behind her, half hoping that Richard was there. But if she'd expected his support she was disappointed. She and Diane were alone together, apart from the child.

'I'm so glad you agreed to come.' Diane pushed a hand through the sun-streaked cap of blonde hair that curved confidingly in at her chin. The action was unstudied, but so elegant that Olivia could only admire her composure. 'Ms Pyatt—or may I call you Olivia?—you probably won't believe this, but I'm hoping we can be friends.'

Olivia felt the hot colour invading her cheeks and despised herself for it. It was Diane who should be feeling uncomfortable here, not her. But Diane was probably used to handling difficult interviews, and she wasn't. Indeed, the other woman's casual approach took her breath away.

'I don't think that's possible, Ms Haran,' she declared now, swinging her tote bag off her shoulder and allowing it to hang from its straps in front of her knees like a shield.

'Well—we'll see,' said Diane, with an enigmatic little smile. She indicated the chair beside hers. 'Why don't you sit down and we'll talk about it? Oh, and call me Diane. Ms Haran is far too formal.'

Olivia drew a breath. In fact, what she really wanted to do was turn around and go back to the hotel. Her anticipation of this meeting had not prepared her for Diane's familiarity, and she wondered now what she had expected from Richard's wife.

But the sun was hot, and she knew she shouldn't take unnecessary risks by standing in its glare. Besides, however surreal this seemed, she had come here to do a job. Unless she was prepared to be sued for breach of contract, she had to do as Diane said and accept the status quo.

Nevertheless, she seated herself on the next but one chair to Diane's, grateful for the shade offered by its striped canopy and the distance it put between them. With her face in shadow, her colour subsided, and she opened her tote bag and extracted her notebook and tape recorder.

Meanwhile, Diane had approached the child again, who was still hanging onto the tiles at the side of the pool. He was a little boy, Olivia saw as Diane lifted him out. Dark-haired and dark-skinned, with a mischievous smile that exposed several missing teeth.

'Go and find your mother,' Diane advised him, after wrapping a fluffy towel about his shoulders. 'My maid,' she added, by way of an explanation as the boy ran off. 'She and Manuel have three grown-up sons. Antonio is their baby.'

'Ah.'

Olivia nodded, making a play of checking that there were batteries in the recorder. But Diane's careless clarification had answered her question. Not Richard's son, but Manuel's.

'Would you like a drink?'

Diane had seated herself again and was regarding her with enquiring eyes and Olivia wondered what she was really thinking. Was this any easier for her than it was for Olivia? Was she really as indifferent to her feelings as she'd like to appear?

'Oh, I don't think—'

'Oh, yes, let's have some coffee.' Without waiting for her guest to finish, Diane got up again and pressed a button that Olivia now saw was set into the wall beside a row of changing cabanas. She came back and sat down again. 'I think we should get to know one another before we start work.'

Olivia rolled her lips inward. And then, putting the recorder aside, she clasped her hands together in her lap.

'You mean, you're going to tell me why you really wanted me to write your biography?' she asked tightly, amazed at her own audacity. She'd never expected to have the courage to challenge her like this.

Diane shrugged. 'You know why I wanted you. I told your agent: I like your work.'

'Have you read my work?'

'Some of it.' Diane nodded. 'I read your biography of Eileen Cusack.' She shook her head. 'I'd never heard of her, you know, but after reading your story of her life I have so much admiration for her.'

Olivia drew a breath. 'You read it?'

'Yes.' Diane looked puzzled. 'Didn't Mrs Goldsmith tell you?'

'Well, yes.' Olivia made a little gesture of dismissal, but that didn't stop the heat from re-entering her cheeks. 'But—people—say things they think you want to hear.'

'People?' Diane gave her an arch look. 'You mean me?'

'Does it matter?' Olivia wished she'd never questioned Diane's statement. 'I—I'm glad you enjoyed the book.' She tried to speak objectively. 'Eileen was a brave woman.'

'Yes, she was.' Diane was thoughtful, but happily the maid arrived at that moment to divert her. 'Coffee and fresh orange juice, please, María,' she ordered pleasantly.

The maid said, 'Yes, Mees Haran,' and departed again.

The heat around the pool was excessive, and Olivia could feel herself perspiring in spite of the thinness of her dress. The cluster of cyprus trees across the pool created a kind of suntrap, and she wondered if the canopy above her was equal to its task.

'Perhaps you think I only invited you here because of Ricky,' Diane remarked after a moment, and Olivia thought how odd the abbreviation of Richard's name sounded to her ears. Indeed, for a moment she wondered if Diane was talking about the same person. 'I didn't—though you've probably realised he's delighted to have you here.'

'Is he?' Rummaging in her bag for a paper tissue to wipe her hot face, Olivia couldn't think of anything else to say.

'You know he is,' said Diane flatly. 'Don't insult my intelligence by pretending he hasn't told you. He's probably already hinted that we're having problems. I know what he's like.'

'It's nothing to do with me,' said Olivia uncomfortably, half wishing Richard had joined them. She wasn't at all sure she wanted to handle this conversation on her own. When she'd contemplated meeting Diane again, she hadn't anticipated that Diane would be so friendly. She was hostile, and she'd expected Diane to be hostile, too.

'If you say so.' Evidently Diane had decided not to pursue it. At least for the present anyway. 'So—' She stretched her legs on the cushioned lounge chair, looking years younger than the thirty-five Olivia knew her to be. 'Tell me how you came to write.'

Olivia shook her head. 'Well, I've always written—' she was beginning awkwardly, when a disturbance on the terrace interrupted them. Another visitor had just arrived: a man, who was exchanging a few teasing words with María. She must have just let him in and she was laughing at something he'd said. Then, as both Diane and Olivia turned their heads, he came casually down the steps towards them.

He was wearing a black collarless shirt under a cream linen jacket and trousers this morning, but Olivia had no difficulty in recognising who he was. She didn't need the other woman's delighted use of his name to remind her, or appreciate the view of Diane as she flew across the pool deck into his arms. As her pulse raced—and her spirits sank almost in counterpoint—she realised that Joe Castellano was apparently a closer friend of Diane's than she'd thought.

CHAPTER FOUR

OLIVIA tore her gaze away from the embracing couple and tried to simulate some interest in the notebook on her knees. Questions, she thought, uncapping her pen; she should make a list of the questions she wanted to ask Diane. Not historical details like what her father did or where she'd been born, but questions about her persuasions: about what she thought of the increase in crime, perhaps, or the proliferation of dangerous drugs.

But apart from jotting down the words 'Guns' and 'Heroin' she couldn't think of anything else to write. Her mind was like a movie screen that was filled with the image of Diane's swimsuited figure melded to Joe Castellano's muscled frame. His legs were parted, and she could see one of Diane's feet stroking his calf, and one brown masculine hand was spread against the creamy skin of her spine.

Suddenly, she was reminded of what Kay had said: that she had heard some other man must have caught her eye. Oh, God! Was that who Joe Castellano was: Diane Haran's lover? When he'd said he was a friend of Diane's, she'd taken him at his word.

If she'd felt hot before, she was fairly burning up now, and it wasn't just the temperature around the pool. She wished desperately that she wasn't there, or that Joe Castellano had chosen some other occasion to announce his return. After the crazy thoughts she'd had about him, she didn't want to meet him again. Not now. If only one of the area's famous earthquakes would swallow her up.

She could hear voices now, and realised that they had separated and were coming towards her. Somehow, she had to get through the next few minutes without betraying how she felt. Should she stand up? Would her legs support her? She couldn't be certain of anything, she thought despairingly. And she probably looked like a sun-dried tomato to boot.

'Joe tells me the two of you have already met,' said Diane without hesitation, and, judging by the openness of her smile, there was no animosity either. And why should there be? thought Olivia, aware of her own imperfections. Compared to Diane, there could be no contest, after all.

'Oh—yes,' she said now, closing her notebook and running sticky fingers over its laminated back. She looked up into his lean dark face and felt her body tingle. 'Um—how do you do, Mr Castellano? How—how nice to see you again.'

He grinned down at her. 'You made it, then?'

'What? Oh, yes.' She licked her dry lips. 'Miss—Ms— Lovelace was very kind.'

'Who, Bonnie?' Joe Castellano laughed, and then to her dismay dropped down onto the footrest of her own lounge chair. 'Hey, if she heard you call her that, she'd blow her top.'

Diane came to stand beside him, running a possessive hand over his shoulder as she spoke. 'Stop teasing Ms Pyatt,' she chided him, evidently not wanting him to be familiar with Olivia's name. Then, as if realising how her actions could be construed, she sank into the adjoining chair. Drawing one leg up to her chest, she rested her chin upon her knee, but her eyes never left him. 'You will join us for coffee, won't you?'

'Coffee?' His dark brows ascended mockingly. 'Something long and cold sounds more like it.'

'A beer, then.' Diane was obviously eager for him to stay.

'A beer.' His mouth compressed. 'It's too early in the day for me.'

Olivia wondered if that was a dig at Richard, but although he could easily have made some comment about the other man he didn't. She wondered if he knew of her relationship with Richard. Had Diane told him that she'd asked her husband's ex-wife to write her story?

'Do you think you're going to like it here?' he asked, turning to Olivia, and she managed not to stumble over her reply.

'It's different,' she said, realising her response was non-committal. 'Do you live in Los Angeles, Mr Castellano?'

'He has a house at Malibu but he lives in San Francisco.' Diane answered for him. Then, as if impatient at the interruption, she attracted his attention again. 'Are you staying for a few days this time?' she asked impulsively. 'I've got so much I want to discuss with you before I leave for the East Coast.'

Joe Castellano shrugged. 'I'd have said you've got your hands full here,' he remarked, his tawny eyes flickering over Olivia's averted head as she struggled to make herself invisible. 'Aren't you pretty tied up with this biography you've decided to have written?'

'I've always got time for you,' Diane retorted, her voice soft and sensual. 'Are you staying at the beach house to-night?'

'Maybe,' he responded carelessly. 'But I want to check in at the hotel. I've got some business meetings scheduled for tomorrow and the beginning of next week, so it may be easier to stay in town. I might spend the weekend in Malibu, though. Why? Do you and Richard fancy joining me for drinks on Saturday night?'

'I—why—' Diane seemed uncertain at first and then, catching Olivia's eye, she seemed to come to a decision. 'Why not?' she agreed lightly. 'So long as Ms Pyatt can come, too.' And as Olivia's lips parted in consternation she added, 'I'm sure she'd love to see the Pacific at sunset. I can get Ricky to play tour guide. What do you think?'

'I'm sure Mr Castellano didn't expect you to ask me—' started Olivia hurriedly, uneasily aware that there was something going on here that she didn't like. What was Diane trying to do? Get her to take Richard—*Ricky*—off her hands?

'Mr Castellano would be delighted if you'd join us,' he interposed easily, and once again Olivia glimpsed the satisfaction in Diane's face. 'But call me Joe, for God's sake! We don't stand on ceremony here.'

'Well...'

'Joe's right,' put in Diane quickly, apparently prepared to be generous if she was getting her own way. 'It's a great idea, Olivia. Joe's house is quite a showplace at the beach. Perhaps you should bring your swimsuit. We could have a moonlight swim.'

Olivia shook her head. She knew she was being manoeuvred into an impossible position and she didn't like it. But she wasn't really surprised. She'd suspected Diane's motives before she left England.

'Trust me—Olivia, right? You'll enjoy it.'

Joe Castellano, at least, seemed to have sensed her ambivalence and Olivia wondered if he knew exactly what Diane was doing. He had to, she decided, her nails digging into her notebook. Why else had he come here the day after he got back?

'I—thought I might do some sightseeing this weekend,' she said stiffly, determined not to be railroaded into acting as Richard's nanny, and Diane gave her an impatient look.

'You'll have plenty of time for sightseeing!' she exclaimed. 'Surely you're not going to turn down the invitation? I thought you'd have jumped at the chance to— to—'

'Spend time with my ex-husband?' demanded Olivia, realising Diane wasn't the only one who could speak her mind. She heard Joe Castellano's sudden intake of breath but she didn't falter. 'I'm sorry, Ms Haran,' she added, getting to her feet, 'but that's not why I came.'

'I was going to say, I thought you would have jumped at the chance to—to speak to people who know me,' retorted Diane coldly. 'You don't imagine we'd have been Joe's only guests, do you? We—he—has lots of friends. You might even have found it interesting to talk to his brother. He's an actor, like me.'

Olivia's face was burning. 'Well, I'm sorry,' she mumbled uncomfortably, 'but I—I don't usually mix business with pleasure.' She licked her lips. 'And—and as Mr Castellano obviously wants to speak to you, perhaps you'd prefer it if I came back at some more convenient time—'

'Oh, for God's sake—' began Diane irritably, only to break off when Joe Castellano got to his feet.

'Cool it,' he said, and Olivia wasn't sure which of them he was talking to. 'I've got an appointment anyway. I won't hold you up any longer.'

'You're not holding us up.' Diane sprang up now, grasping his arm, forcing him to look at her and no one else. 'Don't go,' she cried. 'María's fetching coffee and juice. You can stay for a little while, surely.'

'And be accused of preventing—Ms Pyatt—from doing her job?' he asked, and Olivia didn't know if he was being sarcastic or not. 'I'll ring you later, okay? Give Ricky my regards, won't you?'

'But, Joe—'

Diane's tone was desperate, but he was already walking away. With a casual salute that included both of them, he disappeared into the house, and presently they heard the muffled roar of a car's exhaust.

Silence descended—an uneasy silence that wasn't much improved when Diane turned away and sought the chair she had occupied earlier. Olivia wished she had her own transport, too; that she had the means to get out of there herself. It would be the next thing she'd do, she thought vehemently. Providing she was still employed, of course.

'Oh, sit down, for heaven's sake!'

Diane's impatient command almost had her hurrying to do her bidding, but somehow she stiffened her spine and managed to stay where she was. 'Do you still want to do this?' she asked, half hoping Diane would say no. But she should have known that the other woman wouldn't give up that easily.

'Do I still want to do it?' she echoed, looking up at Olivia with a frustrated stare. 'Of course I want to do it, as you so succinctly put it. That's what I've brought you out here for. If you choose to ruin any chance of a social life you might have while you're here, that's up to you.'

Olivia swallowed, and, hearing the unmistakable sound of footsteps behind her, she sank down weakly onto the chair. She knew it must be María, and she had no desire to arouse her curiosity as well. But she couldn't help wishing that Diane would suggest continuing their interview indoors. It might just be that little altercation with Joe Castellano, but she felt as if her temperature was sky-high.

'Coffee and fruit juice, madam,' said María cheerfully, setting the tray on the low table beside her mistress. 'Would you like me to pour?'

'No, thanks,' answered Diane, dismissing her somewhat ungraciously, and Olivia was aware of the maid's confusion as she hurried back to the house.

Meanwhile, Diane had picked up the pot of coffee. 'How do you like it?' she asked. 'Or do you prefer orange juice?'

'Yes.' Olivia's lips felt parched. 'That is—I would prefer orange juice,' she murmured awkwardly. There were ice cubes floating on the top of the jug and they were a mouth-watering sight.

Diane shrugged, set down the coffee pot again and took charge of the jug. She filled a tall glass and handed it to Olivia. 'You look as though you need this,' she commented drily. 'It may help you to cool down.'

Olivia doubted it, but rather than make any retort she took a generous gulp of the juice. 'It's very hot out here,' she said at last, determined not to let Diane think she could intimidate her. 'If I'd known we were going to work outside, I'd have come more prepared.'

Diane finished pouring herself a cup of coffee, which Olivia noticed she drank without either cream or sugar. 'You'd prefer to work indoors?' she asked, viewing her companion critically. 'I suppose your skin is sensitive. You're like Ricky. You're used to cooler climes.'

Olivia wanted to say that she wasn't like Richard at all, but as she had no desire to bring Richard's name into their conversation again she kept her mouth shut. Besides, she sensed that Diane was only baiting her, and it didn't really matter what she said as long as Olivia didn't respond.

'Tell me how you met Joe at the airport,' Diane invited, changing tack when it became apparent that the other woman wasn't going to rise to her previous lure. She frowned. 'He must have recognised you from your picture on the book about Eileen Cusack.'

Olivia nodded. She had wondered about that, too. She could hardly tell Diane she had been staring at him across the concourse. Had he really recognised her, or had he seen the label on her bag?

'He's quite a dish, isn't he?' Diane went on encouragingly. 'I bet you wondered who he was. I assume he must have approached you. You don't look the type to initiate a pass.'

Olivia put down her glass. 'You're right, of course,' she said flatly. 'Unlike you, I don't covet every man I see. Um—Mr Castellano was very kind, very thoughtful. He could see I was a stranger and he helped me out.'

Diane's lips twisted. 'Believe it or not, but I don't 'covet every man I see' either,' she retorted shortly. 'All right. I know you're still peeved about what happened between you and Ricky, but that wasn't all my fault. It takes two to tango, as they say in Rio. Ricky was ripe for a bit of seduction. I hate to tell you this, Olivia, but *he* came on to *me*.'

'I don't believe you!'

The words were out before she could stop them and Olivia suspected that she'd said exactly what Diane had hoped she'd say.

'Well, that's up to you,' she said now, sipping her coffee and watching Olivia with cool, assessing eyes. 'It doesn't matter, anyway. We've all had plenty of time to ponder our mistakes.'

Olivia pressed her lips together and forced herself to breathe evenly. She would not allow Diane to manipulate her, she thought fiercely, no matter how much she'd looked forward to seeing Richard again. In fact, it was hard to remember now how she'd felt before she left England. Had she really welcomed the news that he and Diane were having problems? Somehow it was difficult to imagine those errant emotions now.

'The relationship you've had—or are having—with your husband is of no interest to me,' she declared, trying to concentrate on what she'd written on her pad. 'Shall we get on with the interview? I'd like to confirm a few preliminary details this morning. Then we can concentrate on the form you want the biography to take.'

Diane's lips twisted. 'I don't believe you, you know.'

Olivia took a deep breath. 'What don't you believe?' she asked, reaching for her glass again with a slightly unsteady hand.

'That you don't care about me and Richard; that you only came here to do a job.' Diane put down her cup with a measured grace. 'You're not that unfeeling, Olivia. I should know.'

Olivia closed her eyes for a moment, praying for strength, and then opened them again before she spoke. 'You don't know anything about me,' she stated firmly. 'It's five years since—since we had any contact with one another, and that's a long time. I've changed; you've changed; we're all five years older. I'm not a junior reporter any more, Ms Haran. I've got an independent career of my own.'

'I know that.' Diane was impatient. 'And I respect the success you've had. That's why you're here, for God's sake!' She broke off and then continued more calmly, 'But don't pretend that you don't still care about Ricky. I don't flatter myself that it was my invitation that brought you here.'

'Well, it was,' said Olivia swiftly, though not very truthfully. It was the chance that she might see Richard again that had overcome her reluctance to work with Diane. But she had no intention of giving Diane that satisfaction, and in any case meeting Richard again had somehow soured that enthusiasm, too.

That—and the startling realisation that she'd been attracted to another man...

'You're lying,' persisted Diane now, leaning forward to pour herself another cup of coffee. But there was no animosity in the words. And before Olivia could attempt to defend herself she went on evenly, 'But perhaps this isn't the time to go into that.' She paused. 'It's Friday tomorrow. I suggest we both take the weekend to think things over, and we'll meet here again on Monday morning.'

Olivia caught her breath. 'You mean—you want me to go?'

Diane shrugged. 'I think it's a good idea, don't you?' She looked at the other woman over the rim of her coffee cup. 'I've got to go into the studios this afternoon anyway, and you'd probably welcome the chance to get your bearings. I suppose I should have realised you can't be expected to work on your first day.'

Manuel drove Olivia back to her hotel, and she was grateful to find that Richard wasn't with him. She needed some time to collect her thoughts before she saw her ex-husband again, and she couldn't help wondering if he knew what his wife was thinking. It seemed obvious to Olivia that Diane's motives weren't as straightforward as she'd have her believe.

She was tired when she reached her room, despite the fact that it was only midday. But her body clock was telling her that it was evening and although she hadn't actually done any work yet her encounter with Diane had taken its toll.

Perhaps she'd done her a favour by suggesting that she take the weekend off, thought Olivia unwillingly, but she doubted Diane had her best interests at heart. No, there was another agenda that only Diane knew about, and while she had been remarkably civil to her Olivia sensed that there was something going on.

An image of Joe Castellano insinuated itself into her mind as she sat down on the side of her bed and kicked off her shoes. Was he really just a friend, as he'd said, or were he and Diane lovers, as she suspected? It was ironic, she thought bitterly, that she and the other woman should be attracted to the same men. But she wasn't foolish enough to think there was any competition between them.

Flopping back on the mattress, she spread her arms out to either side and stretched wearily. The quilt was cool beneath her bare arms and it was so nice just to relax. For the present it wasn't important that Diane was paying for her accommodation. She was too exhausted to care about anything else.

The telephone awakened her. Its shrill distinctive peal penetrated the many layers of sleep and brought her upright with a start. For a moment she was disorientated, not understanding how it could be light outside and she still had her clothes on. She didn't usually need a nap in the middle of the day.

Then, as the phone continued to ring, she remembered where she was and what she was doing. A quick glance at the slim watch on her wrist advised her that it was after half-past four. She'd slept for nearly five hours. She must have been tired. No wonder she felt hungry. She hadn't eaten a thing since early that morning.

Rubbing an impatient hand across her eyes, she reached for the receiver. 'Hello,' she said huskily, but she knew as soon as she spoke who was on the line.

'Liv? Hell, you are there. I was beginning to think you'd passed out in the bath or something. The receptionist insisted you were in your room, but I've been trying this number for hours!'

'For hours?' Olivia blinked. 'Richard, I—'

'Well, for the last half hour, anyway,' he amended quickly, evidently realising it wasn't wise to exaggerate that much. 'If you hadn't answered this time, I was going to come over. I've been worried about you, Liv. Why'd you leave like that without even letting me know?'

Olivia shook her head. She could do without this, she thought wearily, sensing the beginnings of a headache

nudging at her temples. It was the fault of being woken up
so suddenly that was making her feel so groggy. That, and
the emptiness she was feeling inside.

'Didn't Diane tell you why I left?' she asked now, realising he was unlikely to be put off by anything less than
an explanation. 'We—talked, and then she suggested I used
the next couple of days to familiarise myself with my surroundings. I'm seeing her again on Monday morning. But
I'm sure you must know this for yourself.'

'I know what she said,' declared Richard harshly, 'but
that doesn't mean that I believed it. I know my wife. She
looks as if butter wouldn't melt in her mouth, but I know
better.'

'Oh, Richard—'

'I know, I know. That's not your problem.' His tone was
bitter. 'But at least give me the credit for caring what happens to you.'

Which implied that she didn't care what happened to
him, and that simply couldn't be true. For heaven's sake,
before she'd left England she'd believed she was still in
love with him, and it wasn't wholly his fault that she'd
changed her mind. You couldn't be married to someone for
four years without their feelings meaning something to you,
she admitted ruefully. Their marriage might be over but the
memory lingered on.

'I was asleep,' she said now, hoping to avoid any further
discussion of Diane. 'It's the jet lag, I think. I was exhausted when I got back.'

'But—you're all right?' he asked anxiously. 'Um—Diane didn't say anything to upset you?'

'No.'

Olivia was abrupt, but she couldn't help it. She wondered
what exactly he thought she was. She found she resented
the fact that he believed Diane could still hurt her. Had she
given him the impression that she'd spent the last four years
pining for him?

'Oh—good.' He sounded relieved, but she wondered if

he believed her. 'When I found you'd left like that, I was worried in case she'd said something—bad.'

Or incriminating, reflected Olivia, her lips tightening involuntarily. She was suddenly reminded of what Diane had said about him. Was that the real reason for the phone call? she wondered incredulously. Or was she being unnecessarily paranoid? Was he afraid that Diane might have betrayed the fact that he'd destroyed his marriage and not her?

But, no. She blew out a breath. She was overreacting. Richard had rung her, as he said, because he'd been concerned about why she'd left without saying goodbye. It crossed her mind that it had taken him the best part of five hours to express his regrets, but she didn't dwell on it. In the circumstances, it wasn't her concern.

'Diane was—charming,' she said now, although the description barely fitted the facts. But Richard wasn't to know that. He could only take her word for it. And there was a certain amount of illicit satisfaction in assuring him that they had got on so well.

'Was she?' His response was tight. 'Well—don't let that—bewitching façade fool you. Diane's an actress, in every sense of the word. She doesn't know how to be sincere.'

'Richard—'

'I know. I'm doing it again, aren't I? I'm sorry.' His apology sounded genuine, and Olivia sighed. 'In any case, I didn't ring for you to get embroiled in my personal problems. I wanted to ask you if you'd have dinner with me.' He paused. 'I'd really like for us to talk, Liv.'

Olivia stifled a groan. 'Oh—well, not tonight, Richard,' she protested. 'I was thinking of having an early night.'

'Tomorrow, then. Just the two of us. Diane's spending the weekend at the beach. We could have the place to ourselves.'

Olivia didn't know which was worse: the fact that Diane was apparently going to spend the weekend at Joe Castellano's beach house, or that Richard should expect her to dine with him at Diane's. Both alternatives were distasteful to her, but she suspected the former had the edge.

Nevertheless, she would not play into anyone's hands by dining at Diane's house, and she told him so in no uncertain terms.

'I'm—I'm surprised that you would ask me to do such a thing,' she added stiffly. 'I may have to work there, but I don't have to like it.'

'But you said—'

'That Diane was pleasant?' she interrupted him swiftly. 'Yes, she was. But I don't intend to make a friend of her, Richard. Our association is a matter of business, that's all.'

'I understand.' But she doubted he did. 'And I realise it was insensitive of me to suggest that we dined here. It's just a little difficult to make arrangements at such short notice.' He paused. 'I suppose we could always dine at the hotel.'

Olivia's shoulders sagged. 'You mean in the restaurant, don't you?' There was no way she was going to invite him to her suite.

'Unless you can suggest an alternative,' he answered huskily, the insinuation clear in his voice.

'I can't,' she replied, realising that in her haste to avoid a tête-à-tête she had virtually agreed to his suggestion. 'Um—perhaps you ought to ring me again tomorrow. We can finalise the details then.'

Or not!

'There's no need for that.' Evidently he had detected her uncertainty and was not prepared to give her an escape route. 'Look, let's arrange to meet—downstairs in the Orchid Bar at seven o'clock tomorrow evening. If you can't make it, you can always give me a ring.'

CHAPTER FIVE

IT WASN'T until the following morning that Olivia realised she didn't have Richard's number. There'd been no reason for Kay to have Diane's phone number, and she hadn't thought of asking for it herself. She supposed she could contact Diane's agent, but she was loath to publicise the event. And sooner or later she and Richard would have to talk. There was no point in pretending she could ignore what was going on.

Meanwhile, she had the day to herself, and despite the fact that she'd awakened early again she felt much more optimistic this morning. Her first anxious interview was over, and she was determined not to be daunted by anything Diane might say. Instead of using room service, she decided to have breakfast in the terrace restaurant, and after spending several minutes assessing her wardrobe she eventually elected to wear cream shorts and a peach-coloured linen jacket. A thin silk vest, also in peach, completed her ensemble and she secured her hair at her nape with a tortoise-shell barrette.

She thought she looked smart without being too formal, and she assumed she'd struck the right note when the waiter who escorted her to her table gave her an admiring look. 'Just for one?' he asked, his accent faintly Spanish, and she felt her cheeks colour slightly as she nodded.

'I'm afraid so,' she told him half defensively, and was disarmed by his smile.

'No problem, madam,' he told her easily, and led her to a table for two in the sunlit conservatory.

Yet, despite the waiter's reassurance, Olivia was aware that her table drew a lot of curious stares. Perhaps they thought she was someone of importance, she thought, hiding behind the enormous menu. What must it be like to be a celebrity, constantly in the public eye?

Not very nice, she decided, after the waiter had taken her order, and she took refuge in the complimentary newspaper lying beside her plate. Perhaps she should have had room service, after all. Then she wouldn't be feeling such an oddity now.

Still, the food was good, and, ignoring her fellow diners, Olivia succeeded in clearing her plate. She'd not had blueberry pancakes and maple syrup since her visit to New York a couple of years ago, and she refused to count the calories today.

She was finishing her second cup of coffee when a shadow fell across her table, and, glancing up, she found a tall black woman of middle years looking down at her. The woman's hair had been tinted with henna and Olivia was sure she must weigh at least two hundred and fifty pounds. She was stylishly dressed in a navy power suit, with huge padded shoulders and a tightly buttoned jacket.

'Ms Pyatt?' she asked, and Olivia was so taken aback she could just nod. 'Phoebe Isaacs,' the woman added. 'Can I join you?' And, without waiting for an answer, she pulled out a chair and sat down.

Olivia put down her cup. 'How—how did you know who I was?'

'Well, I was gonna ask the waiter,' said Phoebe laconically, 'but as it happens it wasn't necessary. That gentleman over there pointed you out.'

Olivia blinked. 'What gentleman—?' she was beginning, when she saw the man who was seated across the room. He wasn't looking her way at the moment, but his profile was unmistakable. 'You mean—Mr Castellano?' she asked, in a high-pitched voice.

'Yeah. Joe Castellano,' said Phoebe carelessly. 'I gather you've already met him. He often has breakfast meetings here when he's in town.'

Olivia was stunned, as much by the fact that she was seated just a few yards away from the man who had been occupying far too many of her thoughts as by the casual way that Phoebe Isaacs had introduced herself. 'Um—it's very nice to meet you,' she said, forcing herself not to look in Joe Castellano's direction. 'You're Ms Haran's agent, aren't you? Did—did she ask you to come and see me?'

Thoughts that Diane might be thinking of dismissing her were flooding her head, but Phoebe just said, 'Hell, no,' and grinned broadly. She snapped her fingers for the waiter and ordered some fresh coffee. 'I just wanted to meet you for myself. I'm a big fan, Ms Pyatt.'

'Well—thank you.' Olivia would have been flattered if she hadn't felt so flustered, but her awareness of Diane's lover superseded all else. 'I—er—I believe it was you who contacted my agent, Kay—Kay Goldsmith.'

'Sure did.'

The waiter brought a fresh pot of coffee and another cup and Phoebe helped herself before going on. It gave Olivia a moment to register that her accent was different from the ones she'd heard locally. There was a definite southern twang to what she said.

'Anyway, I'm glad you were able to come on out here,' Phoebe continued, after tasting her coffee. 'There's just no way Diane could have packed up and gone to London at this time. What with fittings for the new film, interviews and personal appearances, her schedule is pretty busy. Besides, I dare say you'll be looking forward to a few weeks in the sun.'

'Yes.' Olivia hoped she sounded more enthusiastic than she felt. 'Well—' she swallowed '—it was kind of Ms Haran to invite me. I suppose I could have done most of the research at home.'

'Hey, there's nothing like hearing it from the horse's mouth,' Phoebe assured her lightly. 'And Diane's a generous person, but I guess you know that already.' She paused. 'I understand you've spent the last couple of weeks talking to people who knew her before she was famous. Guess you never found anyone with a bad word for her, isn't that right?'

'Oh—yes.'

Olivia didn't know what else to say, and to a certain extent it was true. But it seemed obvious that Phoebe knew nothing about her previous marriage to Richard. Had Joe Castellano known before she blurted it out? She cast a surreptitious look in his direction. From his gasp he had seemed to be shocked but she suspected he must have known. He was the kind of man who'd want to know everything about the woman he loved.

If he loved her...

Right now, his mind was obviously on other matters. There were three other men at his table and they seemed to be deep in discussion. One of the men was holding forth, waving the bagel he was eating to emphasise his point. Meanwhile, Joe was lounging in the chair beside him, apparently concentrating on what was being said.

Olivia made herself look away. It wasn't as if he had any interest in her, she told herself severely. He'd been polite, that was all, and if he'd noticed her in the restaurant when she hadn't noticed him that was hardly surprising. She was on her own. The waiter had seated her in a prominent position by the window. And she'd attracted a lot of attention, most of it unwanted, she had to admit.

'So—what are you planning to do today?' Phoebe asked now, and Olivia hoped her thoughts weren't obvious to anyone else. The older woman rested her elbows on the table and propped her chin in her hands. Impossibly long nails, painted scarlet, framed her features. 'Diane wondered if you'd like to go shopping. You can get anything you want on Rodeo Drive.'

Olivia took a deep breath. Was that why Phoebe was here? she wondered. Had Diane sent her to look after her, or to ensure she knew exactly where Olivia was? Perhaps she knew Richard had been in touch with her and she was hoping to catch them out.

'Well, I—haven't made any arrangements,' Olivia murmured now. 'I—had thought of sunbathing by the pool.'

'Sunbathing!' Phoebe grimaced. 'Well—I guess if that's

what you want to do. But, you know, I'd be happy to show you around.'

'Thank you.'

Olivia didn't know what else to say, but happily Phoebe had no such problem. 'And is this your first trip to the States?' she persisted, with interest. 'I know your books have been published here, but...'

Phoebe shrugged, inviting Olivia to respond, and, deciding there was no harm in discussing her work, she replied, 'No. It isn't my first trip across the Atlantic. I visited New York about two years ago, to publicise *Silent Song*.'

'*Silent Song*.' Phoebe nodded. 'That was a wonderful book. Diane and I were both touched by the sensitivity you showed in dealing with such a heart-breaking subject.' She smoothed the rim of her eye with one scarlet-tipped finger, as if wiping away a tear. 'I'm sure the Cusack family were real happy with the way you handled their mother's story.'

Olivia pressed her lips together. She wasn't used to such overt flattery, and it was difficult not to show her embarrassment. 'It was a touching story,' she murmured at last, but Phoebe wasn't finished.

'You're too modest,' she said. 'Believe me, I know what I'm talking about. In my job, I represent all sorts of people, and I get to read novels, biographies, scripts, all kinds of stuff. And, girl, let me tell you, you'd be amazed at some of the stuff that gets into print; you know what I'm saying? Stories that are sick. *Sick!* Not inspiring stuff like yours.'

'Oh, well—'

'It's true.' Those scarlet-tipped fingers descended on Olivia's arm. 'Hey, they'll make movies about anything these days; anything that the producer or the director thinks is going to make a stack of bucks.' She gave a disgusted snort. 'Some of them wouldn't know a class piece of writing if it jumped up and bit them on the neck.'

Olivia shook her head. 'I'm afraid I don't know anything about the film industry,' she protested, wondering if Phoebe was aware that her nails were digging into her arm. 'I'm just a writer—'

'*Just* a writer!' exclaimed Phoebe incredulously, her nails digging deeper, and Olivia had to steel herself to stop from crying out. 'Don't put yourself down, girl. You're a fine writer, a fine biographer, a fine human being, I'm sure. Diane wouldn't have wanted you to write her story if that wasn't true.'

Wouldn't she? Olivia wondered, but she didn't voice her doubts about that particular opinion. She was too busy being relieved that Phoebe had withdrawn her hand.

But the reason she'd done so wasn't out of kindness. Olivia was surreptitiously rubbing her arm, trying to get the blood circulating around the slash of whitened flesh where the marks of Phoebe's nails still showed, when she became aware that someone else was standing beside the table. She disliked the fact, but she didn't need the evidence of lean hips and powerfully muscled legs beneath the narrow trousers of his navy three-piece suit to guess who it was. She knew his identity immediately, and although she was forced to acknowledge him the look she cast towards his lazily enquiring face was almost insultingly brief.

Happily, Phoebe had no such reservations. 'Hey, Joe!' she exclaimed, even though Olivia sensed she wasn't altogether pleased at the interruption. 'I thought you were locked in high-level negotiations. Diane said that was why you couldn't have breakfast with her.'

'Does Diane tell you everything, Phoebs?' he asked, and although he used what was obviously Diane's name for her there was a certain trace of censure in his voice. Olivia knew he was looking down at her, but she couldn't bring herself to face him. Which was ridiculous, she thought, when she ought to have been grateful that Diane and Richard were probably splitting up because of him.

'Most things,' Phoebe answered now, unconsciously giving Olivia a few more minutes' grace. 'I know she was disappointed,' she added. 'With you just getting back and all. Still, I guess you've got the weekend, don't you? Plenty of time to catch up.'

'It's good to know you've got my weekend mapped out

for me,' he remarked silkily, but Olivia knew she wasn't mistaken this time: he resented Phoebe's remarks. The amazing thing was that Phoebe wasn't aware of it. Or, if she was, she chose to ignore it in favour of Diane.

'Hey, that's what agents are for,' she said now. 'It's my job to keep Diane happy. You can't argue with that.'

'I wouldn't want to,' he assured her drily. Then, as Olivia had known he would, he spoke to her. 'It seems you've got the weekend off, Ms Pyatt.'

Olivia nodded, and then, because it would have looked odd not to do so, she slanted a gaze up at him. 'That's right,' she said. 'Um—Ms Isaacs has just offered to take me shopping on Rodeo Drive.'

'Has she?' His tawny gaze moved to Phoebe again, to her relief. 'Well, you couldn't be in safer hands,' he remarked mockingly. 'Apart from looking after her clients, there's nothing Phoebs enjoys more than shopping.' His hard face tightened for a moment. 'It was—kind of Diane to make sure you weren't—lonely. I guess this can be a strange and frightening place.'

Olivia clasped her hands together in her lap. Once again, she had the distinct impression that what was being said wasn't the same as what was meant. But she wasn't in a position to query his comments. It was hard enough to think of a response.

'I'm sure I'm going to enjoy my stay,' she declared at last, stung into defending her ability to look after herself. For all she was obliged to acknowledge his concern, she wasn't a child, and she resented being made to feel like one.

'Of course you will,' put in Phoebe before she could continue. 'Diane and I are going to see to that. Don't you worry about Olivia, Joe. We'll see she doesn't come to any harm.'

Joe smiled then, a lazy, knowing smile which, even though Olivia could see had an element of cynicism in it, still had the power to curl her toes. 'I'm sure you will,' he agreed, checking his tie with one brown, long-fingered hand. 'Well, as they say here, be happy!' And, with a nod to both of them, he walked away.

Olivia made the mistake of expelling the breath she had hardly been aware she was holding, and then wished she hadn't when Phoebe's sharp eyes registered her relief. 'Does he make you nervous?' she asked, watching her closely. 'He's a sexy hunk, isn't he? One of a kind.'

'Oh, really, I—'

'You don't have to be afraid to admit it.' Phoebe shrugged her padded shoulders. 'He affects me, too. I guess that's why Diane's crazy about him.' Her eyes narrowed. 'I'm sure you've realised that she and Ricky are all washed up.'

'No, I—that is—' Olivia took a moment to compose herself. 'Are they?' she asked, in a strangled voice.

'Afraid so,' said Phoebe ruefully. 'Which is a pity. Ricky's a nice guy. He just doesn't have what it takes to hold Diane.'

Olivia was tempted to say, Does anyone? But, remembering the way Diane had reacted to Joe Castellano, she held her tongue. 'Um—maybe they'll work things out,' she said instead, trying not to look towards the exit where Joe and his party were just leaving. She dragged her eyes away. 'She—must have loved him when she married him.'

But once again Phoebe had noticed what Olivia was looking at, and after glancing over her shoulder she impaled the other woman with a sardonic look. 'Yeah,' she said, 'but that was a long time ago, you hear? She's older now and—well, wouldn't you choose Joe instead of Ricky—if you had the chance?'

Olivia flushed and concentrated her attention on the table. 'I really wouldn't know,' she denied, wishing Phoebe would go, too. Then, forcing a smile, she summoned the waiter. 'Please,' she said, 'would you put Ms Isaacs' coffee on my bill?'

If she'd thought her action would shut Phoebe up, she was mistaken. 'Why not?' she drawled. 'Let's make Diane pay for my coffee, too.' Then, as if sensing she'd gone too far, she opened her purse, took out a card, and pushed it across the table. 'There, that's my home number as well as the number of my office. If you need anything—anything at all—just give me a call.'

'Thank you.'

Olivia took the card reluctantly, noting almost absently that Phoebe lived in the Westwood area of the city. She knew from the guidebooks she'd read that that was where most of the new Hollywood films were first shown. She wondered if that was why Phoebe had chosen to be an agent, or whether she'd really wanted to star in films herself.

It wasn't important, and Olivia was relieved when the woman pushed back her chair and got to her feet. For a few anxious moments, before Phoebe had given her her card, she'd been afraid she'd been appointed her watchdog. But no. It seemed that now Joe Castellano had gone Phoebe was perfectly happy to leave her to her own devices.

'Have a nice day,' she said, tucking her purse under her arm in a businesslike manner. 'And if you do decide to leave the hotel, grab a cab.'

Olivia breathed a sigh of relief when the woman left the restaurant, and after giving her time to clear the lobby she followed her out of the door. But the idea of sunbathing seemed to have lost its attraction, and she knew it was the knowledge that she was no longer her own mistress that was spoiling her day.

Still, there was nothing she could do about it now, short of packing up and going back to London, and it was silly to let anything Phoebe had said distress her. For heaven's sake, the woman was Diane's agent. She was bound to be partisan. And she'd known Diane and Richard were having problems before she'd left England.

Feeling more relaxed, she glanced around her. The early morning crowds were dispersing, and the boutiques that lined the corridor to the pool and leisure area were beginning to show signs of life. They wouldn't open until later, but that didn't stop her from window-shopping, admiring the silk scarves and exquisite items of jewellery that filled several of the displays.

'You'll have more choice on Rodeo Drive,' remarked a voice that was becoming embarrassingly familiar to her. 'Where's Phoebs? Has she gone to summon Diane's limousine?'

Olivia swung round. 'Ms Isaacs has left,' she declared politely. 'I thought you would have, too, Mr Castellano. I saw—that is, Ms Isaacs mentioned that you were leaving about fifteen minutes ago.'

'And you didn't notice?'

'I didn't say that.' Olivia held up her head. 'Of course I did,' she admitted, half afraid he'd seen her watching him. 'But—I understood you had some business meetings to attend to.'

'*One* business meeting,' he corrected her drily. 'And you'll have noticed that it's over.' He paused. 'So you thought I'd left the building. Or was that what you were told? You know, I guess that's what Phoebs thought, too.'

Olivia stiffened at the implication. 'If you think—'

When she broke off, he regarded her enquiringly. 'Yes? If I think what, Ms Pyatt? Finish what you were going to say.'

'It doesn't matter,' muttered Olivia unhappily, aware that she had been in danger of being indiscreet. 'If—if you'll excuse me, I'm going up to my room. I—er—I've got some work to do.'

'Today?' He sounded disbelieving, and she wondered why he was bothering to ask. It wasn't as if it mattered to him what she did.

'Yes, today,' she said firmly, and saw the cynicism that crossed his lean face at her words.

'And, of course, you don't mix business with pleasure,' he taunted lazily, pushing his hands into his trouser pockets. He rocked back on his heels. 'So there's no point in me offering to take you out.'

'To take me out?' Olivia stared at him, aghast. 'Why would you want to do that?'

'Why do you think?' He shrugged. 'Perhaps you interest me.' His brows lifted mockingly. 'Perhaps I find your candour refreshingly—new.'

'Don't you mean *gauche*?' she demanded, convinced now that he was only baiting her. 'If I accepted your invitation, you'd run a mile.'

'Well, I do that, too,' he admitted modestly. 'Exercise is good for the body.'

Olivia sighed. 'Where I come from, people say what they mean.'

'But I am saying what I mean,' he protested. 'You intrigue me. You do. I don't think I've ever met anyone quite so intriguing before.'

'You don't mean that.'

He feigned hurt. 'Why don't you believe me?' He paused. 'Can't we put the past behind us and start again?'

'Start what again?' Olivia shook her head. 'This is just a game to you, isn't it? Do you flirt with every woman who happens to cross your path? If you do, I can understand why Diane sent that Isaacs woman to keep an eye on you. She probably doesn't trust you at all.'

'No?' His attractive mouth twisted. 'And why should you say that unless you think I really am interested in you?'

'I don't—' Olivia was embarrassed now, and she was sure she showed it. She glanced enviously towards the lifts. 'Look, I've got to go.'

'If you insist…' He seemed to accept her ultimatum and she pressed her lips together nervously as she started across the foyer. 'Oh, Olivia,' he called, just before she pressed the button to summon the lift, and she turned apprehensively towards him. 'Don't believe everything you hear.'

CHAPTER SIX

THE rest of the day was an anticlimax.

Despite her determination not to think about Joe Castellano, Olivia couldn't seem to put him out of her mind. Wherever she went in the hotel, she half expected him to be there, waiting for her, and when he wasn't she knew a sense of flatness she'd never experienced before.

It was stupid, she knew, particularly as their conversation had been so antagonistic, but she'd seemed to come alive when she was talking to him. It was his experience, of course, his ability to make any woman feel as if he was interested in her, but she couldn't remember the last time she'd enjoyed talking to a man so much.

Which was pathetic as well as stupid, she thought later that morning as she lounged somewhat restlessly beside the pool. She was letting a man she knew to be involved with someone else interfere with the reasons she was here. Worse than that, he was the man who was involved with the woman she'd come to study. If she'd taken him seriously, she could have been in danger of blowing her commission as well.

In the event, she decided not to leave the hotel that day, and by the time the evening came and she had to start thinking about getting ready to meet Richard she was almost relieved to have something to do. She could have worked, she supposed, as she'd told Joe she intended to do, but she seemed incapable of concentrating on anything—except images of Joe and Diane in each other's arms...

She decided to wear an ankle-length skirt and wrap-around top for the evening. The skirt was patterned in blues and greens and the crêpe top was a matching shade of jade. It fitted tightly to her arms and displayed a modest cleavage, as well as leaving a narrow band of exposed flesh at her midriff.

She'd washed her hair after her swim as it was inclined to be unruly. It wasn't much more than shoulder-length, but she thought twisting it into a French braid was probably the safest means of keeping it tame. Red lights glinted in its dark gold strands as she secured the braid at her nape, and she was reasonably pleased with her appearance as she checked her reflection in the mirror.

Not that she could hope to compete with Diane's beauty, she admitted as the thing she had been trying to avoid needled back into her thoughts. She couldn't help wondering if Joe would approve of her appearance, and what he'd really meant by accosting her today. Why had he waited? she wondered. What could he possibly hope to gain by playing such a game? Perhaps he enjoyed living life dangerously. She couldn't believe he'd meant what he'd said.

The phone rang as she was stepping into low-heeled strappy shoes that added a couple of inches to her height, and her heart accelerated in her chest. It couldn't be him, she assured herself. Just because she'd been thinking about him it didn't mean she had some kind of extra perception. But her voice was breathy as she said, 'Hello.'

'Liv!'

Her pulse slowed. 'Richard.'

'Who else?' He sounded more cheerful this evening. 'Shall I come up?'

'No.' Her response was unflatteringly swift. 'No, don't bother,' she added quickly. 'I'll come down.'

Richard was evidently disappointed, but he managed to stifle his frustration and only said stiffly, 'Don't be long.'

'I won't be.'

Olivia replaced the receiver, wondering if this had been the wisest move, after all. Wasn't she just playing into Diane's hands whichever way you looked at it? Whether they ate here or at Diane's house, they were still together.

A glance at her watch told her it was still just a quarter to seven. Richard was early, which accounted for the fact that she hadn't been waiting for him in the bar downstairs. Perhaps he'd planned it that way. Perhaps he'd hoped she'd relent, and invite him for a drink in her suite. It must have been quite a blow when she'd said she'd come down.

Whatever, there was no point in keeping him waiting now. There was always the danger that he might take a chance and come up anyway, and it would be difficult to get rid of him if he was at the door.

A final glance in the mirror assured her that if she wasn't exactly glamorous she had nothing to be ashamed of, and after collecting her purse she left the room. But she couldn't get rid of the feeling that she was making a mistake, and she wished she wasn't such a pushover where Richard was concerned.

He was waiting in the lobby, his blond hair glinting brilliantly in the light. She suspected he'd had a root job since she'd seen him the day before, and in a formal shirt and white tuxedo he looked more like the man she remembered.

'Liv!' Once again, he came eagerly to meet her, but this time she was prepared for him and turned her face aside from his seeking lips. 'Oh, Liv,' he muttered huskily, drawing back to survey her, 'you look bloody marvellous! I can't believe I was such a fool to let you go.'

Olivia managed a smile, but she extricated herself from his clinging hands and glanced around. 'Is that the bar?' she asked unnecessarily as the preponderance of orchids should have given her an answer, and he was obliged to nod and accompany her across the foyer.

'I can't believe you're here,' he said, after they were seated on tall stools at the bar. He would have guided her to a secluded booth in the corner, but Olivia had climbed onto a stool before he could do anything to prevent her. 'White wine, right? You see, I even remember what you used to drink.'

Was she so predictable? Olivia considered the point, conceding to herself that her choice of drink hadn't changed in more than ten years. 'Um—I'd prefer a G and T,' she said, even though she rarely drank spirits, and Richard gave her a startled glance before making the order.

'So,' he said, after their drinks were served—Olivia noticing that he'd ordered a double Jack Daniels for himself. He took a swallow from his glass, evidently savouring the stimulation. 'Here we are again. It's just as if we'd never been apart.'

'Not quite like that,' murmured Olivia drily, wondering if Richard had always deluded himself in this way. When they were married, she'd usually deferred to him, so perhaps he was accustomed to her agreeing with everything he said. But he had to realise that she had changed.

'Okay, okay.' He took another generous gulp of his Scotch. 'I know a lot of water's flowed under the bridge since the old days and we've both had time to regret our mistakes. But we're here now and that's important. It shows that something has survived our separation. We might not be able to forget the past, but we can forgive—'

'Richard—'

'I know what you're going to say.' He held up one hand, as if in conciliation, while raising his glass again with the other. Draining it, he handed the empty glass to the bartender, and Olivia realised the gesture he'd made had not been to her. 'Same again, pal,' he ordered, after a desultory check that her glass was still full. 'But believe me, Liv, I've learned my lesson.' He grimaced. 'But good!'

'Richard, I—'

'You're doing it again.'

She frowned. 'Doing what again exactly?'

'Judging me, before you've heard what I have to say.' The waiter brought his second drink, and he took another mouthful before continuing, 'You're not sure if you can trust me. We've just met again, and you're naturally a little nervous. But I swear to God I mean what I say.'

Olivia decided to say nothing. Sipping her drink, she wondered rather cynically if there was anything significant in the fact that Richard had used the same expression as Bonnie Lovelace had done in the car. Well, whatever, she thought ruefully, it really wasn't important any more. If she felt anything for Richard, it was pity, not love.

He was staring at her now, evidently expecting her to make some comment, and she searched her brain for something uncontroversial to say. 'Er—do you come here often?' she asked, licking a pearl of moisture from her lip. 'I must say, it's a beautiful hotel.'

Richard glowered. There was no other word for it. Then he took another huge swig of his drink before going on.

'It's okay, I guess,' he said indifferently. 'It lacks character, but most things do over here. Give me a beamed ceiling and an open fire any time.'

Olivia rolled her lips inwards. 'A beamed ceiling and an open fire,' she echoed disbelievingly. 'This from the man who wouldn't stay in a thatched cottage in case the roof leaked!'

Richard's expression lightened. 'You see, you do remember!' he exclaimed eagerly. 'Our first anniversary, wasn't it? You wanted to see *Romeo and Juliet* at Stratford, and I said *Cats* was more my thing.'

'Yes.' Olivia sighed. 'I guess we were incompatible even then.'

'No—'

'Yes.' She was firm. 'I suppose I just didn't want to see it. Richard, I'll never forget those years we had together, but I don't want them back.'

Richard's expression darkened again. 'Oh, I see,' he said coldly. 'You're going to punish me. It's not enough that I've spilled my guts to you, you're still determined to have your pound of flesh!'

'Oh, don't be silly.' Olivia was impatient. 'I'm sorry if things haven't worked out for you and Diane, but that's not my fault.'

'Did I say it was?' He had already finished his second drink and was summoning the bartender again. 'Fill it up,' he ordered rudely. Then, to Olivia, 'I've ordered dinner for eight.'

'Eight?'

Olivia repeated the words barely audibly, mentally cal-
culating how many Scotches Richard could consume before
then. More than she wanted to think about, she acknowledged, imagining the scene that was likely to ensue. She
had no desire for him to make an exhibition of himself here.

'Yes, eight.' Clearly, his hearing hadn't been impaired,
and when his third drink arrived he reached eagerly for the
glass. He nodded towards her G and T. 'You're not drinking much tonight. Are you sure you wouldn't prefer a glass
of wine?'

'No, I—' What she would have preferred was for him to
go and sober up. She was firmly convinced now that he'd
been drinking before he arrived. 'Um—why don't we go
for a walk? I'd enjoy the exercise. I haven't been out of
the hotel all day.'

'Are you kidding?' Richard looked at her as if she were
mad. 'You can't go walking around the streets at night.'

'It's hardly night—'

'All right. People don't walk here. Except maybe on
Rodeo Drive. This isn't Westwood Village, you know.'

'Westwood?' The name struck a chord. 'Oh, yes. That's
where Phoebe Isaacs lives.'

'Phoebe? Yeah, it might be.' He frowned. 'How would
you know that?'

'She came here. This morning.' Olivia could feel her
cheeks filling with colour, but it wasn't because of Phoebe
Isaacs. 'Um—she joined me. At breakfast. In the restaurant.'

Richard scowled. 'She joined you for breakfast?' He regarded her with suspicious eyes. 'So, you had time for her
but not for me.'

Olivia's lips parted. 'Richard, that was last night—'

'What's the difference?'

'A lot. I was jet-lagged last night.'

'Well, how the hell did she know who you were?'

'My—my picture.' Olivia moistened her lips. 'It's on the
back of all my books.' And then, because she was angry

at herself for hedging, she added, 'And—and Mr Castellano was there.'

'Joe Castellano?' Richard stared at her through narrowed lids. 'You know Joe Castellano?'

'I've met him,' said Olivia uncomfortably, half wishing she hadn't been so honest after all. 'He—er—he was at Diane's yesterday morning.' She hesitated. 'I believe he has some—some investment in her career.'

'Oh, yeah.' Richard was bitter. 'He has an investment all right.'

Olivia took a deep breath. 'How about that walk?' she asked brightly, not wanting to get into a discussion about Joe Castellano with him. 'If—if you think it's unwise to go outside the hotel, we could always go and look at the shops.'

Richard's jaw clenched. 'So, how well do you know this guy?' he demanded. 'Are you saying he had breakfast with you, too?'

'No—'

''Cos I have to tell you, Di won't like that. Hey, did she know Castellano was going to be there? If she did, that's probably why she sent Isaacs along.'

'He wasn't there,' retorted Olivia hotly, but she disliked the thought that Richard should have had the same thought as she'd had herself. 'He—just pointed me out to Ms Isaacs, that's all.' She slid abruptly off her stool. 'Now, are you coming for a walk or not? I do not intend to sit at this bar for another hour.'

'Another half-hour,' protested Richard, but he must have realised she meant what she said. 'Oh, all right.' He finished his drink and got down from his stool, taking a moment to sign the tab the barman slid across to him. 'We'll go and look around the foyer. You can tell me what you think of macho man!'

Olivia's lips tightened. She refused to be drawn into a discussion about Joe Castellano, and she found she resented the fact that Richard should speak so disparagingly of him. And yet, she acknowledged ruefully, perhaps she shouldn't blame Richard. It couldn't be easy for him competing with a man who seemed to be everything he was not.

The shops in the foyer were still open. Their signs indicated that they would be so until ten o'clock. A long day, thought Olivia, recognising one of the sales assistants she'd seen earlier. But the girl was still as immaculately made up as she'd been that morning.

'He's sleeping with her, you know,' Richard persisted, when Olivia stopped to look in a jeweller's window. 'Castellano, I mean. Theirs isn't just a business arrangement.'

'It's nothing to do with me,' said Olivia tightly. 'Um—that ring's beautiful, isn't it? My God, it's fifty thousand dollars! I thought it was five thousand at first.'

'Chicken feed,' said Richard carelessly, scarcely paying any attention to the ring she was admiring. 'Diane spends more than that on her personal trainer, and all he does is supervise what exercise she's taking in the gym.' He grimaced. 'His name's Lorenzo; can you believe it? Lorenzo MacNamara! Isn't that a hoot?'

Olivia blew out a breath. 'If you're going to talk about Diane all evening—'

'I'm not.' Once again, he seemed to realise he was going too far. 'But you can't blame me if I get aggrieved sometimes. And it's so good to have someone—sympathetic—to talk to.'

Sympathetic? Olivia frowned. Was she? She was frustrated, perhaps, and a little resentful that Richard should think she'd be willing to take up where they'd left off, but sympathetic? She didn't know if she was that.

'Anyway,' he continued, tucking his hand through her arm, 'I promise not to talk about Diane and her—well, Castellano, any more. How's that?'

Olivia forced a smile. 'Good,' she said, wishing she could put them out of her thoughts so easily. Instead of which, she spent the remainder of the evening half wishing Richard would tell her what their connection was. Did Joe intend to marry Diane when she was free? Was that an

option? From what she knew of Castellano, she couldn't
see him as anyone's pawn.

By Sunday evening, Olivia had done some preliminary
work on the computer the hotel had supplied for her. She'd
precis-ed her initial impressions of Los Angeles, and typed
out the notes she'd made before she left England. She had
several tapes of interviews, but she'd left them back in
London. She hadn't wanted to take the risk that they might
get lost during her trip.

She'd bought some magazines in the drug store downstairs and spent Sunday afternoon checking for pictures of
Diane. She thought it would be interesting to read another
person's point of view of her subject, but in the event she'd
found nothing of any note. Except an edition of *Forbes* that
featured the brilliant tycoon, Joseph Castellano. Although
she'd despised herself for doing so, she'd bought the magazine and read every word of the article about him.

Which had told her a lot more than Richard had confided.
Although he'd broken his promise not to talk about his wife
several times during the dinner they'd had together on
Friday night, his comments concerning her relationship
with the other man had been judgmental at best. He didn't
like Castellano—which was reasonable in the circumstances. But not every word he'd said about him was true.

For instance, he'd said that Joe was sleeping with Diane,
but there'd been no mention of their association in the article Olivia had read. On the contrary, the woman who most
often featured in the article was someone called Anna
Fellini. They were partners in a winery that was situated in
the Napa Valley.

There'd been lots more, of course: about his investments
in the film industry and banking, and the fact that he owned
a string of luxury hotels. She'd been disturbed to find that
he owned the Beverly Plaza. It was just one of several along
the coastal strip.

That kind of success was overwhelming, and she'd been
glad she hadn't read the article before they'd met. She

would never have dared to say what she'd said to him on Friday morning, she thought, with a shiver of remorse. It was just as well he'd gone away for the weekend.

The last two days had passed reasonably quickly, she acknowledged as she closed down the computer. On Saturday morning, she'd taken a cab to Century City, and spent a couple of hours wandering in what was really an extensive shopping mall. Then, on Sunday morning, she'd visited Rodeo Drive, buying herself some expensive perfume she didn't really need.

She'd taken most of her meals in her room, preferring not to run the gauntlet of open curiosity. Except at breakfast, when she felt less conspicuous, and the waiter, whose name she now knew was Carlos, made sure she always had a table in the window.

She'd missed Henry, of course. When she was working, he often came to sit on the window-ledge beside her, hissing his disapproval when he saw a dog go by in the street. She missed the Harley, too. At weekends, she often took the old machine for a spin.

But, for the most part, she'd been too busy to feel homesick, although she had to admit she was not looking forward to the following day. Having been made an unwilling party to the problems Richard and Diane were having, she couldn't help being influenced by them, and her own association with the man who was causing their unhappiness didn't help.

It was ironic, she thought. She had come here more than ready to take advantage of the situation. Indeed, it had been the knowledge that Richard's marriage was in difficulties that had persuaded her to take the commission. Until then, she'd been adamant that nothing Kay said could change her mind, but the tantalising prospect of comforting the man she'd believed she still loved had swung the balance.

Yet now, after only a few days, she knew that the image she'd kept of Richard over the years wasn't real. Had never been real, she suspected. She'd just made it so. The destruction of her marriage had been so painful, so unexpected, she'd convinced herself that everything Richard had done had been manipulated by Diane. Now, she had to admit to being doubtful. She couldn't believe that Richard had changed that much.

And Diane...

Getting up from the table where she had been working, Olivia stretched her arms above her head and gave a sigh. She didn't like her, she thought, but she could admire her. And perhaps Kay was right. Perhaps this *would* be good for her writing career.

CHAPTER SEVEN

OLIVIA had dreaded going back to Diane's on Monday morning, but in the event her fears proved groundless. A call from Diane's secretary, Bonnie Lovelace, first thing Monday morning confirmed that Manuel would pick her up at nine-thirty sharp, and when she arrived at the Beverly Hills mansion Diane was waiting for her in a sunlit sitting room off the entrance hall.

The sitting room was small compared to the arching atrium, but Olivia guessed her own sitting room would fit into it several times over. It was furnished in limed oak, with chairs and sofas upholstered in flowery pastels, and once again there were flowers everywhere, scenting the cool, conditioned air.

Diane herself was fully dressed this morning, but the businesslike suit of dark blue linen only accentuated her blonde good looks. Nevertheless, she was apparently prepared to treat the interview with all seriousness, and although she greeted Olivia courteously her mind was obviously on other things.

'Please, sit down,' she said, indicating the chair opposite her at a marble-topped table by the flower-filled hearth. 'Did you have a good weekend?'

'I—yes.' Olivia was taken aback by her change of attitude. Gone was any attempt at familiarity, and in its place was a cool politeness that Olivia decided she preferred. 'I—went shopping,' she added, sure Diane wasn't really interested. She would have liked to ask, Did you? but she wasn't sure she wanted to hear the reply.

'Good.' But Diane's response was absent. 'Then, if you're ready, I suggest we get down to work.' She paused, and for a moment Olivia caught a glimpse of the woman she'd met before. 'That is,' she appended, 'if you're still

83

interested in the commission. I realise I haven't given you an opportunity to say what you think.'

Olivia hesitated. *Tell her you can't do it,* a small voice urged her, and she knew this was her last chance to back away. But, although she had the feeling she would live to regret it, some perverse impulse was egging her on.

'I'm still interested,' she said, but her hand shook a little as she removed her tape recorder from her bag and put it on the table. But fortunately Diane didn't appear to notice. Her expression mirrored a satisfaction all its own. Who was she thinking about? Olivia wondered. Richard or Joe Castellano? And once again that small voice mocked her for even having to ask.

Yet, for all that, the next two weeks were productive ones for Olivia. Diane had arranged things so that most of her mornings were free of other commitments, and, although there were occasions when Bonnie Lovelace rang to cancel an appointment, on the whole Olivia's visits were treated with respect.

Olivia soon discovered that, like many women in her sphere of entertainment, Diane enjoyed talking about her childhood. Although it had been far from happy—she pulled no punches when she talked about the stepfather who had abused her—she seemed to regard those years as character-forming. They were past now, so therefore they couldn't hurt her, and if she chose to embellish any of the details there was no one likely to contradict her now.

Her own mother and father were dead, she explained without emotion. Her parents had never been married and Diane had hardly known the Scandinavian seaman who her mother had maintained had sired her. She had died fairly recently, Diane continued with rather more feeling. She'd always neglected herself when her children were young, and although things had been easier for her since Diane became successful she hadn't discovered she had a terminal form of cancer until it was too late.

Diane's brothers and sisters were scattered around the globe, with one of them settled a comparatively short distance away in Nevada. They all kept in touch, she said with some pride, but it wasn't always easy because they had family commitments. She regretted not having any children, she added, but her career came first and she considered she still had plenty of time.

Olivia had wanted to ask her then if Richard had had a part in her decision. Remembering his cruel denunciation of her for not giving him a child, she couldn't believe he'd accepted it without complaint. But perhaps it was enough to be married to an icon. She could hardly compare Diane's situation to hers.

And she reminded herself that she wasn't here to question Diane's lifestyle. It might just be that she didn't consider Richard a suitable father for her child. Of course, Olivia had no doubt about whom Diane would consider a suitable candidate for fatherhood. Although she hadn't encountered Joe Castellano again, she had no doubt that he and Diane continued to see one another on a regular basis.

In any case, she'd found it safer not to dwell on their relationship. Imagining what they did together would have caused her far too many sleepless nights. As it was, it was too easy to let thoughts of him dominate her consciousness, so she did her best not to think about him at all.

She'd seen little of Richard either, which was equally a bonus. According to Diane, he was a keen golfer these days, and his absence from the estate was due to the fact that he'd flown to Las Vegas to take part in a tournament there. In a rare moment of confidence, Diane had hinted that he usually spent more time in the clubhouse than on the golf course, but Olivia had chosen not to comment. She was just relieved that he wasn't around to complicate the situation.

Despite her working schedule, Olivia also found time to do some sightseeing. Her afternoons were usually free, and she'd found she could work just as easily in the evenings. In consequence, she joined several of the organised tours around the area, visiting Disneyland and Universal Studios, as well as the breathtaking beauty of the Orange coast.

She was beginning to feel at home in the hotel, too. Now that she'd become accustomed to its noise and bustle—and she'd stopped being afraid she was going to meet the hotel's owner round every corner—she often booked a table in one of the restaurants, and spent some time people-watching from behind her menu before going up to her room to do some more work.

The hotel certainly attracted a lot of famous people. The main restaurant—the Pineapple Room—was renowned for its excellent cuisine, and Olivia appreciated how lucky she was to be able to dine there every night if she wished. Sometimes, she chose the Bistro, which concentrated on Italian food. And real Italian food, she acknowledged. Not the fast-food variety she was used to eating back home.

It was just as well she didn't have to worry about putting on weight, she thought one evening about three weeks after her arrival. She was sitting in the Bistro, enjoying a luscious pizza with all the trimmings, while the anorexic woman at the next table was picking at a Caesar salad, and sending envious looks in her direction. Olivia thought how awful it must be to be always counting the calories. Did Diane do that? Was that how she stayed so slim?

Her thoughts broke off at that moment. Swallowing rapidly, she put down her knife and fork and stared disbelievingly across the room. Either she was hallucinating, or that was Joe Castellano sitting at a table half-hidden by the trailing greenery. He was alone, she saw; or perhaps his companion had left the table for a few minutes. Either way, he wasn't paying much attention to what he was eating. He appeared to be reading papers from a file that was propped beside his plate.

He hadn't seen her. Or if he had he'd chosen to ignore her. And who could blame him? she mused, remembering how she'd responded the last time he'd spoken to her. She'd been little short of rude and that wasn't like her.

But how was she supposed to behave when a man like him came on to her? It had amused him to make fun of her, that was all, and if she'd fallen for it she'd have been a fool. Of course, he might just have wanted to be friendly and she'd overreacted because of what she knew of him. Surely she wasn't considering Diane's feelings? She would really be a fool to do that.

She looked down at her plate consideringly. If Diane found out he was seeing someone else, what would she do? She didn't appear to care about Anna Fellini, but she was just his business partner. If there was someone else, would her marriage to Richard stand a chance?

She blew out a breath. Not that she owed Richard any favours, but she'd be glad to get him off her back. Joe Castellano's feelings were not her problem. If he was having an affair with a married woman, he deserved everything he got.

She looked up again. Joe hadn't moved. He was still sitting there, scanning the papers he'd taken from the file and sipping his wine. A desolate sigh escaped her. Could she do it? With Diane as a rival, she didn't really stand a chance.

Was he alone? It seemed he was. Stretching her neck in his direction, she could see no evidence that anyone else was dining at his table. The woman at the next table was staring openly at her now and Olivia forced a rueful smile. Did she have the nerve to speak to him? she wondered. And if she did, what did she expect him to say in return?

She took a deep breath. It was ludicrous. For heaven's sake, Richard had left her for Diane and Joe Castellano was infatuated with her, too. What possible chance did she have of attracting his attention? She was tilting at windmills if she imagined she could change his mind.

But... She sighed. She'd never know unless she did something about it. Yet did she really want to get involved in something like this? She frowned. It could be fun, she supposed, but it could also be dangerous. Not just for her peace of mind but because of her career.

Yet she wasn't planning on making a serious commitment, she reminded herself. And it might just save Richard's marriage, after all. And revenge? her conscience chided, bringing a wave of heat to moisten her hairline. She wouldn't have been human if she hadn't thought about that. She sighed. The truth was, her motives were complicated. She wasn't sure what she hoped to achieve.

And she wouldn't achieve anything if she continued sitting here, staring at her congealing pizza, she acknowledged. She glanced down at what she was wearing, wishing she'd dressed with more care, as she did when she dined in the Pineapple Room. Not that her black trousers and cropped black vest were unattractive. But a slinky dress might have helped her to feel more like a *femme fatale*.

'Don't I know you?' As Olivia was trying to summon up the courage to make her move, the woman at the next table, who had been staring at her, spoke to her. 'You're Elizabeth Jennings, aren't you? Oh, this is so exciting! I love the role you play in *Cat's Crusade*.'

Olivia's jaw dropped. 'Oh, no,' she said, hardly able to believe that anyone could have mistaken her for a television personality. 'I'm sorry. You're mistaken. I'm not Elizabeth Jennings, I'm afraid.'

'Are you sure?' The woman had got up from the table she had been sharing with a male companion and approached Olivia's table. 'You're so like her—and you've got an English accent, too.'

'Well, I'm sorry,' said Olivia again, unhappily aware that they were attracting an audience. 'Um—it's very kind of you to say so, but I can assure you I'm not an actress at all.' She pushed back her chair and got to her feet just as Joe Castellano did the same at the other side of the restaurant, and when he turned his head to see what was going on across the room their eyes met.

It was not the way she'd wanted to do it. She'd planned on sauntering by his table and pretending surprise when she noticed who it was. Now, she was caught in the middle of what was rapidly becoming an embarrassing situation. Despite her denials, the woman seemed unwilling to accept the truth.

However, Joe Castellano seemed to sum up the situation

in an instant. Whether he'd heard what the other woman had said, she didn't know, but he didn't walk away. His eyes narrowed for a moment and then, picking up the file he'd been reading, he walked casually towards them. In navy trousers and a matching button-down shirt he looked absurdly familiar—and Olivia had never been so glad to see anyone in her life.

'Olivia,' he said, by way of an acknowledgement, and the woman who had mistaken her for a celebrity produced a frown.

'You're really not Elizabeth Jennings!' she exclaimed as her companion came to join her. 'But you must be an actress. I'm sure I know your face.'

'Perhaps you've seen it on the jacket of one of her books,' remarked Joe smoothly, and the woman's lips parted in a triumphant smile.

'Of course,' she cried. 'You're a writer. Oh, may I have your autograph? I'm an avid reader, you know. I must have read one of your books.'

Joe's brows arched in silent humour as the woman bent to search her purse for a pen and paper, and, meeting his gaze, Olivia felt a surge of excitement herself. It was as if they were sharing more than just this moment, and she decided the woman's intervention hadn't been such a bad thing, after all.

With Olivia's signature on the back of an envelope, the woman was persuaded back to her table, and Joe pulled a wry face as he watched her retreat. 'Sorry about that,' he said. 'We try to ensure that our guests aren't troubled by autograph hunters.' He smiled, and Olivia felt warm all over. 'Though I must admit you do look rather familiar to me, too.'

'Well, I'm sure *she* doesn't know me from Adam,' she murmured modestly. 'I doubt if she's even seen—let alone read—any of my books.'

'Don't underestimate yourself.' His tawny eyes glinted humorously. 'And no one could mistake you for Adam in that outfit.'

'Why, thank you.' Olivia's breath seemed to be caught in the back of her throat. 'That was a nice thing to say.'

'But true,' he declared easily. 'With that tan, you look as if you should be famous, and that's what counts here.'

Olivia bent to pick up her bag. She wasn't embarrassed exactly, but no one had paid her such a compliment before. And then, because she knew she'd never have such an opportunity again, she turned to him. 'If you've got time, perhaps you'd let me buy you a drink.' She hesitated. 'To make up for the way I behaved the last time we met.'

They walked towards the exit together. As he hadn't answered her yet, she didn't know if he wanted her company or not. But once they were outside in the foyer he turned to face her, and she endeavoured to look more confident than she felt.

'You want to buy me a drink?' he queried disbelievingly, and she nodded. 'Hey—what happened just now wasn't your fault.'

'I know that. But that's not the point.' Olivia gripped her bag with nervous fingers. 'Actually, I'd be glad of your company. I don't like going into a bar on my own.'

Joe regarded her intently. 'Do you mean that?'

'Of course.' Olivia licked her dry lips before continuing, 'You can tell me all about this woman, Elizabeth Jennings.' She forced a laugh. 'Being mistaken for her—is it a compliment or not?'

If he was puzzled by her change of attitude, he chose not to show it. 'Okay,' he said. 'You've got a deal, if you'll let me buy you a drink instead.'

'Why not?' She felt a little dizzy with her success. 'Whoever said we had to stop at one?'

The foyer was reasonably quiet at this hour of the evening, and no one took any notice of them as they strolled across to the Orchid Bar. Olivia knew a moment's panic at the thought that Richard might be propping up the bar, but then she calmed herself. So what if he was? she chided. She wasn't doing anything wrong.

Except flirting with the boyfriend of the woman whose

biography she was researching, her conscience reminded
her. This wasn't the way she usually behaved. That was
the truth. But what did she have to lose? she argued impatiently. If Diane chose to sever her contract, so what?

So, she'd go back to England, she acknowledged flatly.
But at least she'd have the satisfaction of knowing she'd
done what she could. To destroy Diane's relationship, or to
save Richard's marriage? she wondered ruefully. She
wasn't absolutely sure, she admitted honestly. And what
about her own self-esteem?

'D'you want to sit at the bar?' asked Joe as they entered
the subdued lighting of the cocktail lounge, but, glancing
about her, Olivia noticed an empty booth against the wall.

'How about there?' She pointed, squashing the memory
of how she'd responded to Richard when he'd made the
same suggestion. And when Joe nodded his agreement she
started across the room.

The booths were cushioned in dark blue velvet and they
had scarcely seated themselves before the waiter was there
to serve them. 'Good evening, Mr Castellano,' he said, and
Olivia wondered if he was surprised at whom his employer
was escorting this evening. 'What can I get you, sir—' his
smile included Olivia '—and madam?'

Joe arched a brow at Olivia, and she said, 'A martini,
please,' as if she never drank anything else.

'A club soda for me,' said Joe, when the waiter turned
to him, and Olivia couldn't suppress a little gasp. 'I've got
work to do later,' he explained, when the waiter had walked
away.

'Work?' Although she'd been taken aback by his decision, Olivia refused to let it daunt her. After all, she didn't
want him to have the excuse that he'd been drunk. She
cupped her chin in her hands and looked at him. 'Isn't it a
little late to be making that excuse?' She moistened her lips
with the tip of her tongue. 'If you didn't want to have a
drink with me, you should have said so.'

Joe's eyes narrowed sardonically. 'As I recall, the deal
was that you should have a drink with me, providing I

dished the dirt on Mrs T—Mrs Torrance, that is. Catherine
Torrance. She's the sexy private eye from *Cat's Crusade*.'

Sexy?

Olivia swallowed the protest that rose automatically to
her lips. 'You mean this Catherine Torrance is the Cat in
the title?'

'And the role that Elizabeth Jennings plays.'

Olivia shook her head. 'And—you've seen it?'

'A couple of times,' he acknowledged. 'It's not bad.'

'And—do you think I look anything like this Elizabeth
Jennings?' Olivia asked curiously, and then coloured at the
look that crossed his face.

'Maybe,' he said, studying her unnervingly. 'I'd have to
know you better before I decide.'

'I meant—in appearance,' muttered Olivia, with some
embarrassment, before realising he was only teasing her
again.

As luck would have it, the waiter returned with their
drinks at that moment, and Olivia took an impulsive gulp
of hers to give herself some Dutch courage. Unfortunately
the gin in the martini was stronger than she'd expected, and
the sharpness of it caught the back of her throat. She had
to swallow several times to stop herself from coughing.
Some seductress, she thought. Did she really think he'd be
deceived by her attempts to appear experienced with men?

'So, how are you and Diane getting on?' he asked, after
a moment, and she guessed he was only being polite. He
must know perfectly well how she and Diane were faring.
Unlike Richard, he hadn't been in Las Vegas for the past
ten days.

'Pretty good,' she replied casually, relieved to hear her
voice sounded normal. She'd been half afraid she'd scraped
her vocal chords raw. But she didn't want to talk about
Diane. That wasn't her objective. 'Um—I haven't seen you
around the hotel for—for a couple of weeks.'

His lips twitched. 'Since that morning you accused me
of flirting with every woman I came into contact with?' he

asked softly. 'Well, no. I went home to San Francisco when my business meetings were done.'

'San Francisco!' Olivia heard her voice rising and quickly controlled it. 'Oh, yes. Didn't—didn't Diane say that that was where you lived?'

'When I can,' he conceded, swallowing a mouthful of his soda. The ice clinked in his glass, and she thought what a pleasant sound it was. But his voice was better. 'In my business, I spend a lot of time travelling. But I'm learning to delegate if I want some time to myself.'

'And do you?' she asked, feeling on safer ground. She picked up her glass and cooled her palms around it. Then she tipped her head and looked up at him through her lashes. 'Want some time to yourself, I mean?'

'Doesn't everyone?' he asked, and although she was feeling more confident his words disturbed her. She had the feeling he knew exactly what she had in mind.

'That depends,' she said, tasting her drink with rather more caution. 'Not everyone knows exactly what they want.'

'Do you?' he asked, relaxing back against the velvet upholstery, and when he stretched his legs she was made aware of how close his thigh was to hers.

What would he do if she touched him? she wondered. If she put her hand on his knee, would he stop looking at her in that teasing way? But what would she do if he covered her hand with his, and moved closer to her? How far was she prepared to go to prove her point?

A finger stroking lightly down her bare arm startled her. 'I guess you don't,' he said huskily, and for a moment she didn't have any idea what he meant. She'd been so intent on her thoughts, so bemused by the notion of getting close to him, that she'd lost the initiative. 'Can I get you another of those?' He indicated her drink. 'I'm going to have another soda myself.'

'Oh—' Olivia was about to say no, and then changed her mind. 'Why not?' she murmured, burying her face in her glass. She needed more time for this to work, she told herself firmly. If she let him go now, she didn't know when she'd see him again.

'Diane said you and Ricky were still married when she met him,' Joe remarked after the waiter had served them, and Olivia stared at him in surprise.

'Yes, we were,' she said, although she would have preferred not to talk about her ex-husband either. 'Um—have you known Diane long?'

'About two years,' he conceded, propping his elbows on the table. He stirred the ice in his glass with one finger and then licked its tip. He was watching her all the time, and she thought how incredibly sexy his action had been. 'How long has Ricky been drinking? Do you know?'

'No.' Now Olivia was defensive. 'He didn't drink when he was married to me. Well—only socially,' she added, forced to be honest. 'You should ask Diane that question. She should know.'

Joe drew the corner of his lower lip between his teeth. He had nice teeth, she noticed, very white with just a trace of crookedness in the middle. 'Do I take it you don't like Diane?' he queried.

'I—neither like nor dislike her,' protested Olivia, and she suddenly knew that was true. She sighed. 'I admit I was doubtful about accepting this commission. But, in the event, I think we get on together fairly well.'

'And Ricky?'

'Richard,' Olivia corrected him. And then, taking another gulp of her martini, she pulled a wry face. 'I think Richard thinks I'm still in love with him. That's why he believes I agreed to come out here. '

'And is it?'

'No.' Olivia was feeling increasingly reckless. 'I'm not in love with anyone right now.'

'There's no special man in England?' Joe asked, meeting her eyes across the rim of his glass. 'You know, I find that very hard to believe.'

'No special man,' Olivia insisted, without hesitation. 'I'd like there to be, but all the men I'm attracted to are either married or involved with someone else.' She licked her lips. 'Like you,' she ventured, wondering if she was drunk or just stupid. 'I think I was wrong about you. You're nice.'

Joe regarded her from between his lashes. 'You'll regret saying that tomorrow,' he murmured, stroking the back of her hand, which was lying on the table beside her glass. 'And I'm not nice, Olivia,' he added softly. 'I'm quite nasty. For instance, I'm tempted to prove you don't mean what you say.'

Olivia blinked. 'How do you know I don't mean it?' she demanded. She looked down at his hand caressing hers and felt the blood surging hotly though her veins. 'And how could you prove it? I'm not an innocent, you know. I have been married.'

'To Ricky,' said Joe mockingly, and she pursed her lips.

'Yes, to Richard,' she agreed, wishing he wouldn't keep talking about him. She blew out a breath to cool her cheeks. 'He's a man, isn't he?'

'Yes.' Joe's fingers touched her knuckles. 'Do you know a lot about men?'

'Not a lot.' Olivia's wasn't drunk enough to lie about something like that. 'Um—enough.'

'From Ricky?'

'From Richard,' she conceded again. Then, because he seemed to be playing with her, she added, 'I suppose it's too much to expect you to show him some respect.'

'Did I say I didn't respect him?'

'You didn't have to.'

'Really?' He frowned. 'Well, as a matter of fact, I don't know him well enough to judge. He tends to act the heavy when I'm around.'

'Do you blame him?'

Olivia was defensive now, and Joe's mouth took on a sardonic slant. 'Well, evidently you don't,' he remarked, withdrawing his hand and breathing deeply. 'Are you sure you're not still in love with him?'

'No.' Olivia wished she hadn't spoken so impulsively. 'I—I feel sorry for him, that's all.'

'Oh.' Joe pulled a face. 'Sorry for him. The death-knell of any relationship.' He gave a humorous smile. 'I hope you never feel sorry for me.'

'As if I would!' Olivia was impatient.

Joe's smile was a little ironic now. 'Why? You don't think I can be hurt?'

'I didn't say that.' Olivia sighed and pressed her lips together for a moment. 'I only meant that you don't really care what I think.'

'Don't I?'

'I don't think so.'

'And you're an expert, are you?'

'No.' Olivia drew her lower lip between her teeth. 'But perhaps I'd like to have the chance to find out.' She caught her breath, shocked at her own audacity. 'If you cared what I think we wouldn't be sitting here arguing about it, would we?'

Joe regarded her impassively. 'What would we be doing?' he asked, but she knew he didn't really expect her to tell him. He was far too sophisticated to respond to her amateur psychology, but, looking at his lean, hard mouth, Olivia knew exactly what she wanted to do.

'I'll show you,' she said, leaning closer, and, cupping her hand against his cheek, she kissed his mouth.

CHAPTER EIGHT

His withdrawal was not flattering. But then, she could hardly blame him for not responding to her advances in a public place. This was his hotel, for heaven's sake. He was probably cringing at the thought that one of his staff might have seen them. How could she have been so stupid? She'd probably destroyed any chance of retaining his friendship, let alone anything else.

'I'm sorry.'

The words spilled automatically from her lips, her head clearing and allowing her to see exactly how foolishly she'd behaved. She desperately wanted to leave, to avoid any further humiliation, but when she would have slid along the banquette to make her escape his hand descended on her knee.

It was funny, she thought, trying to quell her panic. When she'd tried to imagine how he would react if she put her hand on his knee she'd never expected that their positions might be reversed. And his fingers were strong and masculine. She just knew that if she tried to pull away he'd cause a scene.

'Stay where you are,' he said, and the harshness of his tone brooked no argument. 'It's my own fault. I shouldn't have baited you. Though, in my own defence, I have to say I didn't think you'd take me seriously.'

The words 'I didn't!' trembled on Olivia's tongue but she swallowed them back. She would have liked to say something flip and belittling in return, but she couldn't think of anything. And in any case he'd have known it for what it was: a pitiful attempt to redeem her self-respect. So, instead, she told the truth. 'You were right,' she said, with a careless shrug. 'I don't know enough about men.'

Joe's voice was gentler. 'I wouldn't say that.'

'Wouldn't you?' Olivia still couldn't look at him. She looked down at his hand instead, still gripping her knee, and as if he'd just realised what he was doing Joe pulled his hand away. 'I suppose that's because you're too polite.'

'I'm not polite!' he retorted savagely, and then, expelling a weary breath, added, 'For God's sake, Olivia, stop beating up on yourself, will you? It was a kiss, right? Maybe I'm not used to beautiful women making passes at me.'

Beautiful women?

Olivia wanted to laugh, but there was no humour in it. She wasn't beautiful and he knew that. It was just his way of getting out of a difficult situation.

'Please,' she said, and now she turned her head because she wanted to see his lying face, 'don't treat me like a fool!'

'I'm not.' His nostrils flared with sudden impatience, and his strange cat's eyes darkened until they looked almost black. 'Come on.' He took her arm. 'Let's get out of here.'

And do what? she wondered, but she had no intention of staying around to find out. She went with him because she had no choice with his hard fingers circling the flesh of her upper arm, but once they were outside the bar she broke free of him.

'Thanks for the drink,' she said politely, as if there were nothing more between them than a casual acquaintance. 'Goodnight.'

'Wait!'

He caught up with her before she reached the lifts, and she turned to him with what she hoped appeared to be cool composure. 'Yes?'

'Tomorrow,' he said grimly. 'What are you doing tomorrow?'

Olivia's eyes widened. She couldn't help it. 'I—I'm working,' she faltered unevenly, and then despised herself for sounding so weak.

'All day?' he demanded, and she struggled to recover her self-control.

'Why?' she asked stiffly, and, aware that they were attracting a lot of unwelcome attention, he stifled an oath.

'You just work in the mornings, don't you?' he asked, in a low, angry voice, and because she didn't want to embarrass herself any more than she'd done already Olivia nodded. 'Okay.' He took a breath. 'Let me—make amends for this evening's fiasco by taking you to the beach. What do you say?'

Olivia's breath seemed constricted to the back of her throat. 'I—I don't know what to say—'

'Then don't say anything,' he advised shortly. 'I'll meet you here, by the elevators, at two o'clock.'

Olivia licked lips that were suddenly dry with anticipation. 'I—all right.'

God knew why she'd accepted, she chided herself as she went up in the lift to the penthouse floor. But she had and she was going to have to live with it. Or regret it, as the case may be...

When Manuel came to pick her up the next morning, Richard was with him.

She hadn't spoken to her ex-husband for more than two weeks, and she'd come to enjoy the short journey between the hotel and Diane's house. Manuel didn't talk a lot, but he was friendly, and they'd established an easy rapport that was both comfortable and undemanding. Finding Richard lounging in the back of the limousine was not welcome, and she was afraid that her expression showed it.

'Some surprise, eh?' remarked Richard, with obvious resentment at her reaction. 'Foolishly, I thought you might be glad to see me.'

Olivia sighed. 'I am, of course,' she said, without much conviction. 'Did you have a good trip?'

'Oh, you noticed?'

'Noticed what?'

'That I'd been away,' retorted Richard shortly. And then he said to Manuel, 'Get this heap moving, can't you?'

Olivia sucked in a breath and exchanged a helpless look with the chauffeur. She felt embarrassed for Manuel and herself, and she wondered why Richard had chosen to announce his return in this way.

'I knew you'd gone to Las Vegas,' she said now as Manuel drove onto Santa Monica Boulevard. 'Ms Haran mentioned something about a golf tournament.'

'*Ms Haran!*' Richard was scornful. 'You're not still calling her Ms Haran, are you? For God's sake, Liv, her name's Diane. You didn't call her Ms Haran when you first met her.'

'No.'

But Olivia refused to be drawn into a discussion about how they'd met. And, in all honesty, she always thought of her as Diane. But she now never addressed her as anything other than 'Ms Haran'.

'Anyway, I understand you're still working on the biography,' Richard went on disparagingly. 'I'm surprised you haven't been at one another's throats before now.'

'Because of you?'

Olivia's tone was more incredulous than she'd have liked and it inspired exactly the reaction she'd hoped to avoid. 'Why not?' he snarled. 'You haven't convinced me, you know. You didn't come out here just to write a book. You had something else in mind.'

Olivia sighed. 'You can think what you like,' she said, looking out of the window and wishing she'd stuck to her original intention to get herself a rental car. But she'd fallen into the habit of letting Manuel drive her, deciding that it was probably safer as she didn't really know her way around.

'Oh, Liv—' His next words were spoken in an entirely different tone and she prayed he wasn't going to try and rekindle their relationship again. 'I know you despise me for letting myself get into this situation, but have a little pity, will you? I need your support.'

Olivia shook her head. 'I don't despise you,' she protested, but she wondered if that was really true. She blew out a breath. 'I'd like to think we could remain friends.'

'Friends!' His voice rose again. 'Like Diane and Joe Castellano are friends, you mean?'

Olivia hesitated 'I—I don't know what—what Diane and Mr Castellano are,' she murmured unhappily. 'I just meant—'

'Well, I'd like us to be friends that way, too!' exclaimed Richard harshly. 'That way, we'd be together, every chance we got.'

'I don't think—'

Olivia started to say that she didn't think Diane and Joe were together every chance they got and then broke off. She had no desire to have to explain how she felt equipped to make that kind of claim, but Richard wouldn't leave it alone.

'You don't think what?' he demanded, half turning towards her. 'That Castellano and my wife aren't having an affair? Give me a break, Liv. I've got proof.'

Olivia swallowed. 'Proof?' she said faintly, unwilling to admit why she was humouring him in this way.

'Yeah, proof,' said Richard smugly. 'And she knows it.'

Olivia glanced towards the back of Manuel's head. 'Well, I—'

'Does it make a difference?'

Richard's question was urgent, but Olivia felt uncharacteristically blank. 'A difference?' she said, blinking. 'A difference to what?'

'To you and me, of course. To us!' Richard captured one of her hands before she could stop him and brought it to his lips. 'I love you, Liv.'

'Don't say that!' She cast another horrified look in Manuel's direction as she snatched her hand away. 'Richard, please, there is no us! And you know it.'

'I can't accept that,' he declared bitterly. 'I've just not given you enough time, that's all.'

'Time?' Olivia shook her head. 'Time for what?'

'To forgive me,' said Richard doggedly. 'I know you want to.'

Olivia stifled a groan. 'I have forgiven you, Richard, but

that doesn't mean I want you back.' She saw the gates of
Diane's mansion up ahead and moved forward in her seat.
'I'm sorry.'

'You will be,' muttered Richard, flinging open his door
as soon as the limousine stopped, and without waiting for
her to alight he lurched up the steps and into the house,
almost knocking María off her feet.

'Meester Haig is one angry *hombre*,' remarked Manuel
wryly as he helped Olivia out of the car, and she was glad
of his cheerful grin to restore her composure.

'Isn't he though?' she agreed ruefully, looping the strap
of her bag over her shoulder. 'I'm sorry you had to be a
party to that, Manuel.'

'Hey, no sweat,' Manuel assured her as his wife came
down the steps to greet them. 'You're okay, aren't you,
chiquita?' And at his wife's nod he said, 'I see you later,
Mees Pyatt, okay?'

'Okay.'

Olivia gave María an apologetic smile but her mind was
already leaping towards the afternoon ahead. She had the
feeling she was a fool to get any deeper involved in Diane's
affairs than she already was.

As usual, Diane was waiting for her in her sitting room,
but this morning her slim figure was wrapped in the pea-
cock blue kimono she'd apparently donned after taking her
bath. Her hair was still damp and tousled, and the remains
of the continental breakfast she had been picking at were
still in front of her on a tray. As Olivia entered the room,
she flung the script she had been flicking through onto the
floor, her expression warning the younger woman that she
was not in an amicable mood.

'You're late,' she greeted Olivia irritably, though it was
still barely ten minutes to ten. Often, Olivia had to wait
until ten o'clock for Diane to join her. 'I suppose Ricky
was telling you about his trip. I must say, I was surprised
he cleared off to Las Vegas just a few days after you arrived.'

Olivia's fingers tightened around the strap of her bag.

'What Richard chooses to do doesn't concern me, Ms Haran,' she replied, hoping Diane would let it go at that. 'Um—I'm sorry if I've kept you waiting. The traffic was quite heavy this morning.'

Diane pursed her lips. 'But Ricky did go with Manuel to pick you up, didn't he? At least, that's what he told me he was going to do.'

'Well, yes.' Olivia suppressed her frustration. 'Er, shall we make a start? I've got a few queries about what we were discussing yesterday.'

Diane regarded her dourly. 'You're so efficient, aren't you, Olivia? You never let anything get you down. Not an unfaithful husband, or a dead-end job, or the fact that you're living here at my beck and call. How do you do it? I'd like to know.'

'It's my career,' said Olivia tightly, determined not to be provoked.

'And you consider yourself better than me, don't you?' Diane fixed her with a baleful stare. 'Just because you've had a better education. You think women like me are only good enough to sell our bodies to get a decent living.'

'That's not true.'

Olivia had to defend herself, but in all honesty she didn't think of Diane in that way. Not any more. She doubted she would ever like her, but she did admire her. With the background she'd been describing, Olivia considered Diane's success was little short of a miracle.

'But you do despise me.'

'No, I don't.'

'Ricky says you do.'

Richard!

Olivia wanted to scream. 'He's mistaken,' she said firmly. 'Ms Haran, I don't think you're in the mood for working this morning. Would you rather I went back to the hotel?'

'And come back this afternoon, you mean?'

Diane seemed to be considering this, and Olivia wondered what she'd do if she said yes. But perhaps it would be for the best, she thought, remembering her misgivings. She was risking more than her self-respect by playing this game.

'I—I could—' she began, but Diane overruled her.

'No. Joe might come by this afternoon, and I don't want you here if he does.' She frowned. 'I thought he might have come last night, but I guess he heard that Ricky was back from Vegas.' She grimaced. 'I want to ask him about that woman he's been seeing behind my back.'

Olivia felt as if all the colour had drained out of her face. Keeping her head lowered, she sank down weakly onto the sofa opposite Diane. Oh, God, she thought unsteadily, someone must have seen her with Joe last night.

'Cow,' went on Diane expressively, and Olivia stiffened her spine and lifted her head. She wasn't a coward, she told herself fiercely, so she should stop behaving like one. Have it out with Diane now, if that was what this little charade was all about.

But Diane wasn't looking at her; she was thumbing through the pages of a magazine she had at her side. Olivia thought she recognised the magazine. It was the edition of *Forbes* she herself had bought at the hotel.

'What does he see in her?' Diane demanded suddenly, finding the page she'd apparently been looking for and thrusting it across the table at Olivia. 'Have you seen her? Anna Fellini. The woman Joe's mother expects him to marry?'

Olivia stared at the picture of Joe and his business partner with new interest. So their relationship wasn't a platonic one, after all. Her lips tightened. And Diane already had a rival, did she? And one far more adequate to fight for what she wanted than her.

'Well?'

Diane was waiting for her reaction, and Olivia wet her lips as she tried to think of something relevant to say. 'Um—she's very elegant,' she said, not quite knowing what was expected of her. She could hardly denigrate someone who was clearly one of the most attractive women she'd seen.

'Elegant!' scoffed Diane contemptuously. Then, as if revising her opinion, she snatched the magazine out of Olivia's hands. 'Well, yeah,' she said grudgingly. 'I suppose she is sophisticated, if you like that kind of thing. But she's not hot. She's not sexy. She doesn't turn on every man she meets.'

'No, I suppose not.' Olivia had to admit that Anna Fellini's looks were not sensual. Hers was a more classical appeal. Straight blunt-cut hair that shaped her scalp, and a Roman nose to die for. She guessed that, like Joe's, her predecessors had been Italian. Which was probably why his mother would approve of the match.

'I wonder if she's come to LA with him?' Diane brooded. 'He was due back from San Francisco yesterday afternoon.' She scowled, and looked at Olivia. 'I guess you think I'm crazy, don't you? As if he'd prefer a tight-assed bitch like her to me.'

Olivia didn't know what to say to that. 'Maybe he was busy,' she offered, apropos of nothing at all. Then, in an effort to change the subject, she asked, 'Did you find those photographs of when you were a teenager that you were going to show me?'

Diane tossed the magazine aside, her shoulders slumping gloomily. 'No,' she said impatiently. 'I forgot all about them, if you want to know. Ask Ricky where they are. I don't see why he shouldn't make himself useful. I'm going to take another shower and get dressed, just in case Castellano decides to show.'

Olivia made no attempt to find Richard after Diane had gone up to get changed. The idea of asking her ex-husband for anything, after the conversation they had had earlier, was abhorrent to her, and she had enough to worry about as it was. Not least the arrangement she had made to meet Joe that afternoon. When she'd agreed to his request, she'd never considered how he might spend his morning. The thought that he could turn up here at any moment caused a feeling of sick apprehension in her stomach.

Oh, she was no good at intrigue, she told herself crossly. Last night—well, last night she had had too much to drink, as witness the aspirin she'd had to take to ease her headache this morning, and what had happened seemed like some crazy dream. She couldn't believe that she'd behaved so outrageously. Did she really need this kind of hassle? Wouldn't it be simpler if she finished the book at home?

Of course it would, but for all that she knew she wasn't eager to do it. Well, not yet, she amended, reluctant to think it through. For all her fears—her anxieties about Diane's reaction—it was a long time, if ever, since she'd felt such excitement. She was tempting fate, maybe, but she'd never know until she tried.

Diane came back about forty-five minutes later with Bonnie Lovelace in tow. Olivia hadn't been aware of the other woman's arrival, but she'd learned from experience that Bonnie was often at the house. 'I've decided you two can work together this morning,' Diane announced, to Olivia's dismay. She checked her hair in the mirror and admired the shapely curves of her figure. In a cream silk dress piped with red that flared from the hips and swirled some inches above her knees, she looked delightfully cool and svelte. 'I'm going to try and find a date for lunch at Spago's,' she declared confidentially. 'Tell Ricky not to bother to wait up.'

'I will.'

Bonnie simpered; but then Bonnie always simpered when she was around Diane, thought Olivia irritably. But she couldn't help a twinge of envy that Diane could just take off without even an apology. She grimaced. She should have known it was going to be one of those days when she'd found Richard waiting in the car.

CHAPTER NINE

IT WAS nearly half-past one by the time Olivia got back to the hotel.

She felt tired and frustrated, aware that most of the morning had been a waste of time. As usual, Bonnie had taken her responsibilities seriously, and although she'd paid little attention to anything Olivia had said she'd managed to talk continuously for almost two hours.

Diane had apparently suggested that she should show Olivia the photographs she'd been asking about earlier, and to Olivia's dismay she had produced a box which must have contained every photograph Diane had ever had taken. And, ignoring Olivia's protests, she'd insisted on staying with her, poring over her shoulder, and discussing them at length.

Olivia's head had been aching when Bonnie seemed to realise the time, and she'd turned down Bonnie's offer to have lunch at the house. Not that she expected Joe to turn up after Diane's rather obvious announcement. But she'd desperately wanted to get away from the other woman's nasal tones.

It was deliciously cool in her suite, and someone had placed a bowl of cream roses on an end table by the sofa. Their delicate fragrance eased her tension immediately, and, noticing the card that was attached to them, she turned it over.

'To an English rose,' she read disbelievingly, and the handwriting was not Richard's.

Her heartbeat quickened. There was only one other person she could think of who might send her roses, and she glanced hurriedly at her watch. A quarter to two, she thought, feeling a twinge of panic. If the flowers weren't a form of compensation, then she'd never be ready in time.

Dropping her bag onto the Chinese rug, she took a can of Diet Coke from the freezer and popped the tab. He wasn't coming, she assured herself, drinking thirstily. There was no reason for her to worry about the time.

But what if he did?

The thought was irresistible, and without giving herself the opportunity to have second thoughts she scooted into her room. A quick shower, a change of shirt, and some fresh lipstick, she decided firmly. Even if he didn't turn up, she had to eat.

She was downstairs again at a minute past two. In a bronze short-sleeved shirt and the black Bermudas she'd worn earlier, she looked cooler than she felt. The hair at her temples was damp and it wasn't because of the hasty shower. She was sweating with nerves and wishing she'd had time to eat something to settle her stomach.

He wasn't there.

Well, she hadn't expected him to be, she told herself grimly. Diane hadn't gone out that morning, dressed to kill, in order to have lunch with her accountant. No; Olivia had known exactly where she was going. Castellano might be playing hard to get, but Diane had his number—in more ways than one.

All the same, Olivia couldn't help a feeling of disappointment. Even though she'd virtually convinced herself that he wouldn't be here before she came down, somewhere deep inside her she'd sustained the fragile hope that she might be wrong. But she wasn't. It was nearly ten minutes past two and there was no sign of him. She was wasting her time hanging about here. She should just forget all about Joe Castellano and go and get herself some lunch.

'Ms Pyatt?'

The voice was male, but unfamiliar, and the brief spurt of anticipation she'd felt upon hearing it died. She swung round to find a tall man who looked strangely familiar staring at her. But she didn't know anyone in Los Angeles, she thought crossly. It was possible that with that muscular build he was a celebrity she'd seen on television. But if so, how had he known her name?

'Yes,' she said at last, reluctantly, trying desperately to remember where she'd seen him before. She supposed he could work in the hotel. Was he a bodyguard, perhaps?

'Sorry I'm late,' he went on easily. But when she still looked blank he explained. 'I'm Benedict Jeremiah Freemantle, Mr Castellano's personal assistant.'

B.J.

Olivia's lips parted in sudden comprehension. Of course, that was where she'd seen him before. He'd been with Joe at the airport. She'd seen him on the day she arrived.

But what was he doing here? she wondered. Had Joe sent him to make his apologies or what? She didn't like the idea that Castellano should have someone else to do his dirty work for him. Why couldn't he have just picked up the phone?

'Mr Castellano had to fly to San Francisco this morning,' he continued, his gesture inviting her to accompany him towards the exit. 'But he'll be back by the time we get to the house. If you'll come with me, Ms Pyatt, I'll take you to him. He was very sorry he couldn't come to meet you himself.'

'Wait!' Olivia realised she had obediently fallen into step beside him, but now she came to an abrupt halt in the middle of the foyer. 'The house?' she echoed, not understanding him. Her pulse quickened. 'You mean Ms Haran's house in Beverly Hills?'

B.J.'s stocky features shared an equal lack of comprehension now. 'Ms Haran's house?' he echoed, as she had done. 'No. I'm to take you to Mr Castellano's house in Malibu.'

'Oh!'

Olivia's lips formed a complete circle, and B.J. gave her a slightly wary look. 'You were planning on spending the afternoon with Mr Castellano?' he queried. 'I was told you knew all about it.'

'Oh, yes.' Olivia hurried into speech. 'Yes, I did.'

But Joe's house in Malibu! she thought, her pulse accelerating. She'd certainly never expected he'd take her there. He'd invited her to the beach and she'd foolishly taken him at his word.

'Good.'

B.J. was looking considerably relieved now, but she wondered how he'd react if she said she'd changed her mind. She wasn't entirely convinced of the sense in behaving so recklessly. Yet, after last night, what did she have to fear?

The car waiting outside was nothing like the limousine that took her to and from Diane's. It was a dark green sports saloon with low sleek lines and broad tyres. A thoroughbred, she thought, in every sense of the word.

B.J. made sure she was comfortably seated before walking round the car to get in beside her, and Olivia was intensely conscious of her bare knees below the cuffs of her shorts. She should have worn a skirt or trousers, she thought, trying to limit the exposure. But B.J. barely glanced at her before starting the engine of the powerful car.

The car drew a certain amount of attention, but Olivia guessed the man beside her drew some as well. B.J. was thirty-something, blond-haired, and undeniably good-looking. A Californian beach boy, she mused, but it was hardly an original thought.

'So how are you enjoying your stay in Los Angeles?' he asked, after they'd negotiated the ramp onto the freeway, and Olivia forced herself to consider what he'd said. So long as she didn't think too much, she thought she'd avoid any pitfalls. It was thinking about Joe that caused her so much stress.

'Um—very much,' she answered after a moment, covering her knees with her hands. 'I've never been to the West Coast before so I've done a lot of sightseeing.' She stopped, realising she was sounding like a tourist. 'When I wasn't working, of course.'

B.J. cast her an amused glance. 'Of course.' He swung

the wheel to overtake a vehicle on the nearside and Olivia's fingers tightened automatically. She still wasn't used to this style of driving, but the manoeuvre was accomplished without incident and she relaxed. 'Have you met anyone interesting yet?'

'Interesting?' Olivia's shoulders lifted. 'Do you mean someone famous or just—well, anyone?'

'Aren't the two descriptions mutually exclusive?' asked B.J. drily and then laughed when she gave him a worried look. 'Just joking,' he added, but she wasn't sure he was. Like his employer, he seemed to enjoy mocking the establishment.

To her relief, Olivia found the scenery a more than adequate substitute for her thoughts. Beyond the hills north of Los Angeles, the tumbling surf of the Pacific had a wild, untrammelled beauty. Inland, the twisting canyons where the rich had their homes only gave way to the chaparral-covered slopes of the state parks, while along the shoreline the miles of inviting beaches were practically deserted.

'Have you ever been surfing?' B.J. asked as the sun glinted on the gleaming shoulders of two men, lying out in the bay, waiting for the big wave to ride their boards into the beach, and Olivia shook her head.

'No,' she admitted. 'I'm not even a particularly strong swimmer. But I expect you are.' She paused, and then added nervously, 'Does—er—does Mr Castellano go surfing, too?'

'Only on the Internet,' replied B.J. ruefully. 'He's usually too busy to waste time having fun.' He glanced her way. 'Except on special occasions,' he said, grinning at her. 'You'll have to teach him to relax.'

Olivia stiffened. 'I don't think I could teach Mr Castellano anything,' she said, alert to any insinuation. 'I don't know Mr Castellano very well as it happens. But I expect you know that. You were there when we met.'

'Yeah.' B.J. gave her another studied look, and then nodded his head. 'Yeah, I was,' he repeated, with a curious

inflection to his voice. 'I guess you don't know Mr
Castellano at all.'

Olivia barely had time to consider what he might mean
by that before B.J. took an exit ramp for the Pacific coast
highway that curved down towards the gleaming waters of
Santa Monica Bay. The road curved around a headland
where flowering broom and cyprus trees screened the
ocean, and then the iron gates of a private estate appeared
on their left.

An octagonal-shaped gatehouse that B.J. carelessly announced had once been a mission chapel stood beside the
entrance, but no deferential retainer hurried out to open the
gates. Instead, B.J. inserted a plastic card into a slot beside
the mailbox, and the gates opened automatically to allow
them through.

Despite the fact that Diane had called it a beach house,
Joe's sprawling residence bore little resemblance to the
kind of place Olivia had expected. An image of a clapboard
house, with a wrap-around porch, and deckchairs under the
awning, suddenly seemed so inadequate. At least she didn't
have to worry about their isolation, she thought ruefully. It
must take an army of staff to run an estate like this.

Yet, for all her misgivings—and the still lurking belief
that she shouldn't have accepted his invitation—Olivia was
enchanted by her first sight of the house. Nestling on a bluff
of land, overlooking its own private stretch of beach, it was,
quite simply, breathtaking.

Like the gatehouse, the first impression she got was of
an octagonal building, with an uninterrupted view of the
ocean. But as they drew closer she realised that it was a
kind of conservatory she could see, and that the single-
storey dwelling itself was reassuringly rectangular in shape.

But there were windows everywhere, each with its own
set of shutters. Square windows, round windows, and oriel
windows in the glass-walled conservatory. The shutters
were painted black and were a stark contrast to the white-
painted walls, while the double doors that stood wide
looked solidly substantial.

Another car stood on the crushed-shell drive: an open-topped convertible that was clearly built for speed. 'You can relax, he's back,' said B.J. cheerfully, but Olivia wasn't so sure. As her pulse quickened and her knees turned to jelly, she wondered if she'd ever relax again.

It wasn't until she was getting out of the car that another worrying thought struck her. What would she do if Diane was here? She'd said she was going to find Joe, so why not come out to the house? It was possible, she thought apprehensively. Anything was possible in this totally unreal environment, and she licked her lips rather anxiously as B.J. sauntered round the bonnet of the car.

'Go right ahead,' he said, indicating the open doors, and as they crossed the forecourt she was intensely conscious of the noise their feet were making. It seemed inordinately intrusive, and she wondered if it was a good or bad sign when Joe didn't come to meet them.

The entrance hall briefly distracted her attention. The high ceiling was inset with a row of skylights that cast bars of sunlight down across the veined marble floor. Urns, overflowing with flowering plants and shrubs, provided oases of colour and delicate sculptures in ebony and bronze were set against the walls.

There were paintings on the walls too, mostly modern pieces, she thought, that blended well with their surroundings. It would have been impossible for the place to look cluttered. It was far too spacious for that, the walls a neutral shade of oyster beige, with earth-toned rugs to give the room depth.

'He's probably in the den,' said B.J., dismissing the maid who came to meet them and crossing the hall with the familiarity of long use. He started down a long gallery, whose windows were screened against the sun, bidding her to follow him, and despite the screening the whole place had an open feel to it, with tall archways on either side inviting further exploration.

Olivia heard Joe's voice before they reached the den, and the withdrawal she felt at knowing they weren't going to be alone was tempered by her reaction to his voice. It was so familiar to her, and she knew she ought not to be so aware of him. She was doing this for Richard, she told herself fiercely, but the words had a hollow ring.

The den was at the back of the house and, in spite of her nerves, Olivia's first impression was of light and space. Once again, the room was dominated by the windows that overlooked the ocean, the book-lined walls and leather-topped desk barely registering when compared to the view.

But it was the man seated behind the desk, his booted heels propped indifferently on a corner of the polished wood, who instantly drew her eyes. In a cream silk shirt and the dark trousers of a suit, the jacket of which was thrown carelessly across the desk, his only concession to informality was in the fact that he'd removed his tie and loosened his collar. Yet, for all that, he looked just as attractive as ever, particularly so when she realised he was alone and merely talking on the phone.

His dark brows arched ruefully when she and B.J appeared in the doorway, and, swinging his feet to the floor, he got abruptly to his feet. 'Yeah,' he said, to whoever he was talking to. 'I'm sorry about that, too. No. No, I'm afraid that won't be possible. Um—well, maybe, later in the week.'

It was obvious he was trying to get off the phone, but when B.J. mimed that they would go away again he shook his head. 'Stay,' he mouthed. And then, into the receiver, he said, 'Oh, of course. I am, too. I'll speak to you soon. Yeah. Right.'

He hung up with obvious relief, his face lightening as he turned to his guests. 'Sorry about that,' he said, raking back his hair with a weary hand. 'I've not even had time to change.'

'Well, I'll get back to L.A.' said B.J., saluting his employer good-naturedly, and Joe nodded gratefully as the other man turned to go.

'Thanks,' he said, and Olivia felt a little shiver slide down her spine. So they were to be alone, then, she thought uneasily. She'd half hoped that B.J. would be around to drive her back to the hotel.

B.J. sauntered off, his deck shoes making little squeaking noises on the marbled floor. Olivia hadn't noticed the sound when they were coming here, but then her heart had been thundering in her ears. Now, the silence was oppressive, and she wondered if Joe was wishing she hadn't come.

He sighed suddenly, his breath escaping from his lungs in a rush, and Olivia couldn't help flinching at the sound. 'So,' he said, as if aware of her state of tension, 'will you excuse me while I go and take a shower?'

'Of course.'

Olivia was only too pleased at the prospect of having a few moments to herself. She needed the time to get used to the luxury of her surroundings; to come to terms with the unwilling emotions that seeing him again had aroused.

'Good. Good.' Joe looked at her a little too intently for a minute. 'You're okay with this, aren't you?' he asked, his eyes narrowing. 'As you turned me down before, I suppose it was slightly autocratic bringing you here to the house.'

'It's okay.' Olivia knew she had to handle this, and behaving like a shrinking violet was not going to do any of them any good. 'It's fine,' she added, when he still continued to stare at her. 'Do you mind if I go outside?' A safer option? 'I'd like to look around.'

'No problem.' Joe came round the desk, and although her instincts were to retreat she stayed where she was. 'I'll show you the way,' he said, halting beside her. 'Perhaps you'd like to take a swim. There's a pool in back that gets sadly underused.'

'I'll—er—I'll just look around for now,' Olivia murmured tensely, her skin warming at his closeness, prickling with the awareness of his powerful frame. She forced herself to look up at him. 'Perhaps we could both swim later. I don't like swimming alone.'

'Don't you?' There was a wealth of experience behind those two words, and she was sure he knew exactly what

she was trying to do. The strange thing was, he was letting
her get away with it, and she pondered his motives for
doing so. 'Well, we'll see,' he conceded now, and to her
relief he moved towards the door. 'D'you want to look
around the house first?'

Olivia's jaw dropped. 'The house?' she echoed faintly.
'But—I thought you were going to take a shower.'

'I am.' His mouth twisted. 'I'm not suggesting you join
me. I just thought you might like to find your way around,
that's all.'

Olivia swallowed. 'All right.'

'Right.' His eyes slid thoughtfully over her determinedly
smiling face, and then he shook his head. 'Right,' he said
again. 'Follow me.' And Olivia squared her shoulders as
she trailed him out into the gallery.

They turned away from the entrance hall this time, passing through what appeared to be another reception room
before entering an enormous room on their right. Here a
cathedral-like ceiling with more of the signature skylights
spread light over what seemed like acres of polished wood,
with curving armchairs and hide sofas in cream and beige
and brown.

Like the entrance hall she had seen earlier, the colour in
the room came from plants and flowers, with an enormous
Chinese carpet occupying the centre of the floor. There
were glass-topped tables and tall lamps with bronze shades,
and a stately baby grand against the far wall.

But it was the light streaming in through wide sliding
doors that drew Olivia into the room, and without waiting
for Joe to accompany her she stepped outside. Only not
outside, she saw at once. Instead, she was in the octagonal
solarium she'd seen as they'd driven up to the house, with
the blue sweep of the bay all around her.

'D'you like it?'

Apparently prepared to delay his shower indefinitely, Joe
lingered in the doorway, his arms crossed over his chest.
His cuffs were turned back and the hands he had been running through his hair had left it ruffled and standing on end

in places. Yet for all that he was still the most disturbing man she'd ever seen.

'It's—incredible,' she said, speaking impulsively at last. 'I don't know what I— Well, I never expected anything like this.'

'I like it,' he declared simply, propping one shoulder against the frame of the door and crossing one ankle over the other. 'It used to belong to an old movie actress, believe it or not, but that was many moons ago. She'd dead now, sadly, but they say she used to love this place. When it came on the market, I made an offer.'

'That they couldn't refuse, I'll bet,' said Olivia without thinking, and Joe's mouth compressed into a rueful smile.

'You could say that,' he conceded. 'Do you blame me? When you want something, you don't hang around.'

Olivia moved towards the long windows. 'Is that your credo in life, Mr Castellano?' she asked lightly. 'If you want something, go for it, no matter who gets hurt?'

'The woman was dead—'

'I know.'

'But you're not talking about Lilli Thurman, are you, Olivia?' His voice roughened. 'If you're talking about yourself, that's a whole different ballgame.'

CHAPTER TEN

'MYSELF!' Olivia had bent one knee on the cushioned window seat that circled the solarium to enable her to look down at the beach, but now she lowered her foot rather jerkily to the floor. 'I don't know quite what you mean,' she said, and meant it. She wasn't in any danger of hurting anyone—least of all him.

'If you say so,' he said, cupping the back of his neck now with both hands and stretching the muscles of his spine. His eyes turned towards her. 'Why did you come?'

Olivia's throat felt tight. 'Why did you invite me?'

'Good question.' His arms fell to his sides and he straightened away from the door. He regarded her from beneath his thick straight lashes. 'Perhaps I was curious to see how far you intended to go.'

Olivia stiffened. 'Perhaps that's why I came, too,' she declared coolly, refusing to let him see that he'd disconcerted her. She paused. 'Do you want me to go?'

'No.' But his response was harsh, and although his gaze moved down over the betraying contours of her breasts to the slim bare legs below her shorts the brooding darkness of his expression made her think he was having some trouble with his feelings as well. He took a deep breath. 'I guess this is where I go take that shower.'

'If you must,' she said recklessly, and although he had turned away her words brought him to an ominous halt.

'What's that supposed to mean?' he demanded, looking back at her over his shoulder.

'It doesn't mean anything.' But Olivia was suddenly aware of how easy it was to heighten the tension here, and the knowledge excited her. She ran a provocative tongue over her upper lip. 'Unless you want it to, of course.'

'Don't,' he said abruptly, turning fully to face her. 'Don't even think about it.'

'Think about what?' she asked innocently. 'I haven't done anything.'

'Not yet,' he retorted harshly, one hand balling into a fist at his side. His mouth twisted. 'It doesn't suit you, Olivia.'

It was a deliberate insult, but she chose not to let it upset her. She sensed that Joe had only said it to try and take charge of a situation that was running beyond his control, and although he could have meant what he said she'd never have a better chance to put her own sexuality to the test.

'Doesn't it?' she countered now, turning sideways so that the sun profiled the upward tilt of her breasts and lifting the moist hair from her nape. 'So what does suit me, Mr Castellano? Saying nothing? Doing as I'm told? Letting other people walk all over me?'

'No one's walking over you!' exclaimed Joe tightly, and when she arched a mocking eyebrow he demanded, 'Well, who is it? Not me, that's for sure.'

'Aren't you?' She didn't know what was driving her to say these things; she only knew she felt compelled to go on. 'You feel sorry for me, don't you, Mr Castellano? Go on. Admit it.'

'I don't feel sorry for you,' he grated between his teeth. 'For myself, maybe.' He raked back his hair with a hand that wasn't entirely steady. 'Why are you doing this, Olivia? You're not really interested in me.'

Her breath caught in the back of her throat. 'Aren't I?' she asked faintly, and then took a gulp of air when he uttered an oath and came towards her.

He halted directly in front of her, the scent of his male sweat mingling with the warmth in the room to create a potent mixture. 'Stop this!' he ordered angrily. 'It's gone on long enough, do you hear me? I don't know what the hell you think you're playing at, but I think you've forgotten I'm no green youth and you're definitely no *femme fatale*!'

Olivia winced. He certainly didn't pull his punches, and
what had been an exciting game suddenly became an embarrassing confrontation. He wasn't amused, that was obvious, and she had to steel herself not to flinch when he
thrust his face towards her.

She was breathing shallowly, nonetheless, and in spite of
her efforts to appear unmoved by his deliberately cruel
words she was forced to take a step backwards, her hand
raised in an involuntary gesture of defence. No one, not
even Richard, had ever made her feel so small, but she
refused to let him see what he'd done.

'Do you always attack things you can't deal with?' she
demanded tensely, hoping he couldn't hear the tremor in
her voice. 'If I didn't know better, I'd say you were afraid
to show your emotions—or afraid *of* them, perhaps.'

Joe glared at her. He was breathing rapidly, and the
movement of his chest caused a curl of dark hair to appear
in the opened neckline of his shirt. She could see more of
his chest hair, outlined beneath the fine cloth of his shirt,
and she concentrated on this to avoid looking into his grim
face.

'You don't know what you're talking about,' he said
savagely, and she felt a ripple of anticipation feather her
skin. She was right, she thought incredulously. She had
upset his cool self-control. Whatever reason he'd had for
inviting her here, she'd confounded him, and she felt a little
burst of power at the thought.

'Don't I?' she said now, holding her ground with difficulty nevertheless. The urge to move away from the ag-
gressive inclination of his body was tempting, but she
wouldn't give him that satisfaction. 'How do you know?'

'For God's sake, Olivia—'

With an angry exclamation, he raised his hand to push
her away from him. Or, at least, that was what she thought
he'd planned to do, judging from the fury in his face. But
although his fingers connected with her body just below
her shoulder they curled into the soft fabric of her shirt,

bunching it into a ball, and using the leverage to jerk her towards him.

Her breasts thudded against his chest, but although she clutched at him for support he made no attempt to put his arms around her. What was happening here was no gentle flirtation but a primitive demonstration of sexual domination.

'Take my word for it,' he said in a low voice, his hot breath filling her nostrils, 'this is not a good idea!'

She believed him.

Trapped against him as she was, she had a whole different slant on the situation, and while there was something infinitely appealing about the muscled strength of his body crushing her breasts she doubted she would sustain any credibility if he attempted to call her bluff.

'All right,' she said, lifting her hands from his waist and pressing them against his chest. 'All right, I believe you.' But when she tilted back her head to look into his face she saw not anger there but raw frustration.

'Dammit,' he said harshly, his fingers releasing their hold on her shirt only to slide over her shoulder. They tightened over the narrow bones, probing and kneading her taut flesh. 'Dammit, Olivia, you shouldn't have started this!' And his other hand came up to cup the back of her neck.

There was a moment when she had the crazy thought that he was about to strangle her, but his touch was possessive now, not violent. His fingers slid inside the neckline of her shirt, cool against her hot skin. His breathing was still rapid, but its heat was no longer threatening, and she was mesmerised by the narrowed tawny eyes that seemed to be searching every inch of her upturned face.

Then he lowered his head and kissed her.

His lips brushed hers, once, twice, coaxing her lips to part, and then took possession, his tongue slipping between her teeth. Olivia swayed against him, and any thought of resistance was forgotten beneath the all-consuming pressure of his mouth. His mouth was incredibly soft, incredibly hot, and incredibly sensual, robbing her of any opposition and turning her quivering limbs to water.

The impact of his kiss flowed down into her stomach, leaving her breasts tingling and flooding her loins with heat. Her knees felt weak, uncertain, and between her legs a pulse throbbed with an insistent need. She couldn't ever remember feeling so sexually aroused, or so powerless to hide the way she felt.

His hand slid down between them, popping the buttons on her shirt and exposing the lacy stitching of her bra. His fingers insinuated themselves into the bra, finding the swollen nub of her breast. He rolled the hard bud between his thumb and forefinger, and she arched against him urgently, helpless to hide her desire.

And as she did so she became conscious of his shaft, hard against her stomach. Thrusting against the taut line of his zip, it was a blatant advertisement of his own arousal. As if she needed any proof, she thought dizzily as the hand that had been massaging her nape slipped down her back and cupped her bottom.

His hand didn't feel cool now; it felt hot, the heat burning through the thin cotton of her shorts. She knew the craziest urge to release the button at her waist and send the shorts tumbling down to her ankles. She wanted his hands on her flesh, she realised madly. She wanted to feel his hot skin against hers...

When he abruptly let her go, she was totally unprepared for it. One moment her palms had been flat against his shirt, her thumbs probing between the taut buttons, her nails scraping his hair-covered chest, and the next he was propelling her away from him at top speed. Rough hands captured the two sides of her shirt and dragged them together, and as he struggled to fasten the buttons again Olivia realised it had come free of her shorts and she was displaying a bare midriff as well.

She tilted back on her heels, grateful for the window-seat that supported the backs of her knees as she endeavoured to regain her balance. But although she brushed his hands away and fastened the shirt herself she couldn't look at him. She was too afraid of what she'd see if she looked into his face.

The silence was ripe with recriminations. Although neither of them spoke at first, Olivia was overwhelmingly aware of the emotions they were both trying to control. Dismay, on her part, and an aching sense of shame at her own stupidity, and bitterness, she thought, on his, and disgust at what she'd made him do.

'I'm sorry,' she got out, at last, as he was turning away from her, and he swung round almost violently, piercing her with a savage look.

'Don't,' he said, somewhat ambiguously, and she wasn't sure whether he meant that she shouldn't apologise or simply not speak at all. He heaved a breath. 'Like I said before, I need a shower. Can you—entertain yourself while I go and get out of this suit?'

Olivia nodded, not trusting herself to speak, and without another word he left the solarium. She heard him cross the vaulted living room and then the sound of his footsteps died away along the gallery beyond. Only then did she sink somewhat weakly down onto the cushions behind her and give way to a shuddering sigh.

What had she done?

As the possible consequences of her behaviour swept over her, she propped her elbows on her knees and pushed her fingers up into her hair. She hadn't had time to braid it before she left the hotel, so she had secured it at the back of her head with a leather barrette. Now, though, the moist hair was escaping, partly because of her own actions and partly because Joe had dislodged the barrette. The strands that curled down around her fingers made her suddenly aware of how she must look. With her shirt loose and her mouth bare of any lipstick, she suspected no one could have any doubts as to what had been going on.

'Are you all right, madam? Can I get you anything?'

As if her humiliation wasn't yet complete, Olivia lifted her head to find the maid she and B.J. had seen on their arrival hovering by the sliding glass doors. Had Joe sent her to check on her, she wondered, or was the woman acting purely on her own initiative? She was obviously curious about what had been going on, and Olivia could have done without those intent dark eyes assessing her appearance.

'I—' The impulse to ask the maid to call her a cab, to leave before Joe returned from taking his shower, was tempting, but she suppressed it. She wasn't a coward, she told herself severely. And she had nothing to be ashamed about. Well, not much, she conceded grudgingly. 'Um—' She swallowed. 'Do you think I could have some tea?'

'Tea?' That had clearly not been high on the maid's list of expectations. Vodka, perhaps; or something stronger. But tea? However, she managed to contain her reaction, and added politely, 'Of course. Would that be with milk or lemon, madam?'

Olivia sighed again. 'Milk, please,' she said, refusing to be intimidated. But she was relieved when the woman departed, even if she wished she'd asked her where the bathroom was as soon as she'd gone.

Getting up, she glanced ruefully about her. It was just as well that the beach was private, she reflected, making an attempt to tuck her shirt back into her shorts. She hadn't chosen the most appropriate place to conduct her big seduction scene. She grimaced. Some scene; some seduction! After the way he'd behaved when she'd tried to kiss him the night before, she should have known better than to try again.

And yet he had sent her the roses...

The roses!

Olivia groaned. She'd been so disconcerted by her own reactions at seeing Joe again that she'd forgotten all about the roses. Dear Lord, he probably thought she was pig ignorant as well as everything else. All the same, she couldn't help wondering why he had sent them when he obviously had no interest in her.

Well, not of a sexual nature anyway, she amended, pacing rather agitatedly about the room. Unless sending roses was to him just a formality. He'd probably asked his secretary to send them. The wording might even have been her idea as well.

She didn't know what to think, and that was a fact. For a man who had two women in his life already, he showed an extraordinary lack of loyalty to either. He was having an affair with Diane at the same time that Diane was telling her his mother expected him to marry Anna Fellini. And although she didn't kid herself that he'd been in any danger of succumbing to her charms there had been moments when he was kissing her that she'd sensed he was close to the edge.

She lifted both hands and smoothed them over her hair. She definitely needed a bathroom, she fretted, before he came back and found her like this. She wanted to renew her make-up and comb her hair and try and restore some semblance of composure.

Picking up the purse that she had dropped earlier, she ventured somewhat tentatively into the living room. Looking about her, she was once again charmed by the uncluttered beauty of her surroundings, and although the temptation was to linger she forced herself to go on.

Cool marble floors stretched in either direction when she stepped out into the gallery. Mentally tossing a coin, she turned to her left, pausing at every open doorway, hoping to find what she was looking for.

The size of the house was staggering. She glimpsed a dining room and several sitting rooms before gazing aghast at an indoor pool. Several archways opened into the pool room, and she saw it had a sliding roof that could be opened to the sun. And, like all the other rooms, the view from the long windows was extensive, this time looking out on a palm-fringed patio, with sloping lawns and terraces leading down to the shore.

But the pool room seemed to mark the end of the gallery, and, retracing her steps, she felt a twinge of panic quickening her feet. Joe had said she could look around but she still had the feeling she was intruding. But, dammit, where were the bathrooms in this place?

The truth was she'd hoped to tidy herself before the maid returned with the tea. What kind of guest allowed herself to get into such a state without even knowing the layout of the house? The woman was curious enough about her as it was.

Deciding that perhaps one of the sitting rooms might have a mirror at least, she entered the first room on her right. Like the rest of the house, it was exquisitely—though in this case austerely—furnished, with dark mahogany furniture and a pair of sofas upholstered in dark orange suede.

But there were no mirrors here. The walls were hung with more of the modern paintings she had seen in the entrance hall. But open double-panelled doors indicated that there was another room beyond this, and, squaring her shoulders, Olivia crossed the bronze patterned rug that was set squarely in the middle of the polished floor.

She paused in the doorway of a large bedroom, which, like the sitting room before it, had a decidedly masculine air about it. The walls were a dark gold in colour, and the huge carpet was essentially a shade of burnt umber, with a huge colonial bed whose solid head- and baseboards enclosed a king-sized mattress spread with a dark gold quilt.

Olivia's lips parted in some confusion. There were clothes draped over the end of the bed, and now she became aware of it she could hear water running some place close at hand. In the adjoining bathroom, she realised belatedly, though the knowledge didn't answer her needs. Dear Lord, she thought, this must be Joe's bedroom. The water she could hear running was from the shower.

Panic paralysed her. Of all the bedrooms in the house she had had to choose his. If he discovered her here, he was bound to think she'd come looking for him. Would he believe her if she said that simply wasn't the case?

Her brain kicked into action. There was absolutely no reason why he should find her there, she reminded herself impatiently. He didn't even know she'd left the solarium, after all. All she had to do was scoot back along the gallery to the living room. She could even take a chance and investigate one of the other sitting rooms. There were bound to be suites of rooms that were not occupied.

She would have turned away then had not a photograph on a bedside table caught her eye. The picture was of a woman; she could see that from the doorway. But the woman's identity was hidden. The frame was turned slightly too far towards the bed.

The water was still running, and although she knew it was nothing to do with her Olivia couldn't resist finding out whose picture he kept beside his bed. Was it Anna Fellini's, or Diane's? She couldn't believe it was the latter, when he'd invited Richard as well as Diane to the house.

It was neither. Inching the picture round with the tip of her finger, Olivia saw that the woman in the photograph was much older than she'd thought. Elegant, still, with long, slender limbs and a coil of night-dark hair secured to the back of her head, her resemblance to Joe was unmistakable. She guessed this was his mother. How discriminating of him to keep her picture beside his bed.

'Ah, you are here, madam.'

Once again, the maid's supercilious voice startled her into action. Olivia swung round hurriedly, desperate to stop the woman from saying anything more—and knocked the photograph off the table.

It tumbled noisily to the floor. Olivia snatched it up at once, miming for the maid to go away. 'I'm coming,' she mouthed, grateful to see that the glass in the frame wasn't broken, but even as she set it back on the table Joe himself opened the bathroom door.

The maid had disappeared now, any idea of pretending not to understand Olivia's silent pleas quickly suppressed. She knew when to make an exit, thought Olivia, wishing she had known the same. As it was, she was left to stare at her host, his shoulders streaming with water, his hips swathed in a hastily wrapped towel, his frowning countenance a mirror of his discontent.

'Olivia!' he said, not without some frustration. 'What the hell's going on?'

CHAPTER ELEVEN

'WHERE did you disappear to yesterday afternoon?'

Diane posed the question the next morning as Olivia was enjoying an unexpected cup of coffee prior to starting work. Usually, Diane wanted to get straight down to business as soon as Olivia arrived, but this morning she'd chosen to offer the younger woman some refreshment first.

Was it a coincidence? Olivia wondered, praying her pink-tinted cheeks wouldn't give her away. But it was odd for Diane to show any interest in what she'd been doing, when she normally preferred talking about herself.

Olivia expelled a breath as the memory of the previous afternoon came back to her. Had she really visited the house at Malibu? Had she really talked herself into Joe Castellano's arms? Had she really stood in his bedroom and stared open-mouthed at his towel-clad figure? God, she'd wanted to die when he'd emerged from the bathroom and found her poking about in his room.

But of course she hadn't, even though the memory still caused a quivering in her stomach. People didn't die, not from mortification anyway. That would have been much too easy a solution to being caught.

'I was looking for a bathroom,' she'd said, aware that her explanation wasn't convincing him. 'And—and then I saw that picture and—and—'

'Wanted to see who it was?'

'Well, yes.' Olivia had chewed her lip. 'I suppose you think I was being nosy. It's—it's your mother, isn't it? She looks a lot like you.'

Joe's expression had grown sardonic. 'I'm not sure if she'll regard that as a compliment or not.'

Olivia had coloured at his sarcasm, and sought desper-

ately for an alternative. 'And—well, I forgot to thank you
for the roses, too.'

'The roses?'

She'd known as soon as he said the words that he knew
nothing about them, and she'd hurried into speech to rescue
her gaffe. 'I mean—the hotel, of course,' she'd muttered,
though she couldn't believe they would have put such a
message on them. 'Um—I'm sorry for the intrusion.' She'd
backed away towards the door. 'I'll see you later on.'

Thankfully, he hadn't pursued it, and she'd been left with
the uneasy suspicion that Richard must have sent them,
after all. It was the kind of thing he might do, and she'd
been foolish to give Joe Castellano the credit. Just because
she hadn't recognised the handwriting... How stupid that
seemed now.

But then, she reflected, she seldom thought sensibly
when he was around. And even now, sitting in Diane's
sitting room, the image of his lean, muscled torso, with its
triangle of coarse dark hair arrowing down to his navel,
was still disturbingly vivid. The towel, knotted carelessly
about his hips, had exposed the bones of his pelvis, but
she'd been hotly aware of what it had concealed. After all,
only minutes before, he'd been moulding her body to his
thrusting maleness, and the sensuality of what had happened between them was too acute to be denied.

She couldn't ever remember feeling that way with
Richard. The sex they'd shared had been satisfactory
enough, she supposed, but there'd been none of the excitement that being with Joe had aroused. Excitement, and a
wholly sexual awareness, she acknowledged tremulously.
She'd been aware of herself as well as him, and of the loss
his withdrawal had made her feel.

But, obviously, he hadn't felt the same. Despite the fact
that there'd been moments when she was sure he had lost
control of his emotions, common sense had prevailed. But,
whatever loyalties he had, he was only human, and when
she'd thrown herself at his head he'd been tempted.

But not for long...

Olivia had found a bathroom without the maid's assistance. She'd decided it would be too humiliating to ask the woman something which would prove she'd had no right to enter Joe's suite of rooms. It had been easy enough, as it happened. The door further along the gallery had opened into another bedroom suite. With every possible amenity in the bathroom, she'd noticed tensely, including cut-glass jars of creams and crystals, and exclusive bottles of perfume for a guest's use.

But what guest? she'd wondered ruefully as she'd viewed her own dishevelled appearance in the mirror. Not someone like her, who looked and behaved as if she'd never seen a naked man before. Dear Lord, what must he have thought of her stumbling around in his bedroom like a schoolgirl on her first date? She'd been married and divorced, for God's sake. What was there about this man that made her act in such a way?

Yet, although she'd been quite prepared for him to come back and say he'd called a cab to take her back to the hotel, he hadn't. Even though, when he'd returned to the solarium to find her wolfing down the plate of muffins the maid had provided with the tray of tea, he must have felt like it. Instead, he'd gone to stand by the windows, giving her some privacy to empty her mouth. And then, when he'd thought it was appropriate, he'd suggested that she might like to join him for a walk on the beach.

Olivia had finished the muffin before replying, deciding that to explain that she hadn't had any lunch would imply an eagerness to get here she didn't want to convey. 'That sounds inviting,' she said, trying to sound casual as she licked a crumb of chocolate from her lips. She gulped the remainder of her tea and glanced behind her. 'I'm ready if you are.'

'Are you sure?'

There was a trace of humour in his expression as he turned away from the windows, and she was instantly aware that his tawny gaze missed nothing. But it was too late now to make an explanation, and she dabbed her mouth with a napkin, and got to her feet. 'I'm sure.'

'Okay.' He gestured towards the sliding doors. 'Let's go.'

She was intensely conscious of his presence as they walked back along the gallery. In denim cut-offs and a cotton polo shirt, he seemed more approachable than before. His bare feet were slipped casually into a pair of worn deck shoes, and no one meeting him for the first time would have imagined the commercial power he possessed.

Commercial power?

She chose not to examine that thought too closely, and when she passed the door to his suite of rooms again she deliberately looked away. She was glad of the sight of the pool room to give her something to talk about, and Joe explained they had cool days even in southern California.

In the event, they went out through the pool room onto the patio at the side of the house. From here, it was possible to see that the land shelved down to the shoreline in a series of terraces, with tree-covered slopes and tumbling waterfalls breaking up the view.

'Oh, it's so beautiful!' said Olivia impulsively, turning her face up to the sun. 'I can't believe you call this a beach house. If I lived here, I'd never want to leave.'

'Is that so?' His tone was sardonic, and she realised she had spoken childishly again. 'Well, it is a house, and it's at the beach,' he murmured mildly. 'I like it, too, but I also like my house in San Francisco. It's cooler there, so I guess I have the best of both worlds.'

Olivia nodded, managing a tight smile, but she was warning herself not to make any more mistakes. He was humouring her; she knew it; she was almost sure now he didn't want her here. He would have preferred to send her packing, only he'd decided to disarm her first.

They walked down through the gardens, Joe pausing every now and then to point out some rare flower or to draw her attention to the view. And, although she had determined to be on her guard with him, his manner was persuasive. It was so easy to believe he was having fun.

The air was magic, a combination of exotic plants, a Pacific breeze, and warmth. In normal circumstances, Olivia wouldn't have been able to wait to dive into the ocean. The anticipation of how that cool water would feel against her hot skin was almost irresistible.

A long wooden dock jutted out from the shore, and Joe explained that he had a boat moored at Marina del Rey. Although he was reticent about its size, Olivia guessed it would be elegant. If there was one thing she had learned about him from his house, it was that he had exquisite taste.

They spent some time on the dock, watching the waves curling under the boardwalk, and then strolled companionably along the shoreline, their shoes making a trail in the wet sand. And although Olivia had promised herself that she wouldn't get swept away again by his charm and influence she found she was talking about her work without restraint.

She'd realised later that he was probably skilled at gaining people's confidence, at introducing certain topics and drawing them out. But at the time she wasn't thinking; she was just flattered by his interest, and this was one area, at least, where she felt at ease.

'So what made you decide to write Diane's story?' he asked at last, after expressing his sympathy at the tragic death of Eileen Cusack. 'I mean—' For once, he was diffident. 'I'd have thought she was unlikely to accept your motives. You were her husband's ex-wife, after all. It could have been a recipe for disaster.'

'Why?' Olivia frowned, glancing up into his lean, intelligent face with curious eyes. Then, because she found it difficult to sustain his gaze, she looked away. 'In any case, it was Diane who asked me.'

'You're kidding!'

'No, I'm not.' Olivia felt vaguely indignant now. 'I admit, I was surprised at first, but it's been okay.'

'But she couldn't be sure your motives were genuine.

When you accepted the commission, I mean,' he added swiftly. 'How did she know you hadn't changed your mind?'

'Changed my mind?' Olivia was confused. She shook her head and several wisps of hair that had escaped from the braid she'd fastened so hurriedly earlier floated about her face. 'Changed my mind about what?'

His mouth tightened and she sensed her reply hadn't pleased him, but his voice was mild when he spoke. 'I'm sure you know,' he said. 'You told me yourself that Ricky believed you were still in love with him. You might have wanted him back. That was always a possibility, but I guess Diane cared more about your reputation as a biographer then the inherent dangers to her marriage.'

'Now wait a minute…' Olivia halted now, her reluctance to get involved in any more controversy muted by a very real need to understand. She brushed back her hair with an impatient hand. 'Diane has nothing to fear from me.' She blew out a breath. 'Whatever she's told you, Richard means nothing to me.'

'Do you mean that?'

Olivia felt the heat invading her neck. 'Of course I mean it.'

'But you don't deny you're not still with the man you left Ricky for?'

'The man I left him for?' Olivia was indignant. 'I didn't leave Richard for a man!'

She thought he paled slightly at that, but before she could elaborate he spoke again. 'The—woman, then,' he said harshly, a line of white appearing around his mouth. 'The—the person you said you'd fallen in love with.'

Olivia gasped. 'Are you implying that—?'

'You said there was no special man in England,' Joe reminded her doggedly, and she stared at him as if she couldn't believe her eyes.

'And that made you think—' She broke off, and then continued, unsteadily, 'There is no special man, but there's

no special *woman* either. I didn't leave Richard for anyone.
He left me!'

'But Di—that is, I thought—'

'Yes? What did you think?' Olivia found she was shaking with anger now. 'I'm sorry to disappoint you, but I wasn't the guilty party. Unless the fact that Richard thought I was *dull*, and I couldn't produce any children, constitutes a breach of the marriage contract in your eyes!'

Joe's jaw dropped. 'Then—what—?'

'Oh, ask Diane,' muttered Olivia disgustedly, striding back along the beach. Her eyes were smarting with unshed tears, but at least she now knew what Diane was telling everyone. No wonder she'd had no objections to Olivia's coming here. She'd probably told her friends that Richard had invited her.

Joe caught up with her before she reached the place where the dock acted as a breakwater to the incoming tide. He looked frustrated, and although she was hot and angry she realised she could hardly put the blame on him. 'I'm sorry,' he said, his lean frame blocking her path to the terrace. 'I realise this must be painful for you. I'd no idea that Ricky wanted a divorce.'

Olivia took a deep breath. 'It's all right—'

'It's not all right.' He regarded her with doubtful eyes. 'Look, it's probably my fault. I've—misunderstood the situation. I guess your coming out here— Well, you must admit it is unusual. But if Diane asked you—'

'She did.'

'Then I apologise.'

Olivia shrugged. 'It doesn't matter.'

'It does matter.' He sighed. 'Look, this must be bloody painful for you.'

'No.' The last thing she wanted was for him to feel sorry for her. 'It isn't painful at all. I admit I thought it might be. But it's not.'

Joe frowned. 'So you're not still harbouring some great passion for him?'

'For Richard?' If she hadn't felt so emotional, she might

have laughed. 'No.' Then, because she was afraid that if he continued looking at her like that she'd make a fool of herself again, she glanced at her watch. 'Gosh, is that the time? I really ought to be getting back.'

She thought he looked as if he would have liked to object, but it was probably just wishful thinking on her part. And, when he moved aside, she started up the path. She forced herself to walk slowly, even though her nerves were urging her to rush madly back to the house and call a cab. She hoped he wouldn't offer to drive her back to the hotel. She badly needed some time alone.

She saw the Harley when she was crossing the grassy slope that led up to the patio. She hadn't noticed it when they left the house because she'd been too busy admiring her surroundings, but it was propped on its stand, a few feet from the windows of the pool room.

She halted in surprise and Joe walked on a couple of steps before realising she wasn't with him. 'That's—that's a Sportster, isn't it?' she exclaimed, gazing at the motor-cycle with undisguised admiration. And although she'd been desperate to leave before its gleaming frame reminded her nostalgically of home.

Joe's brows arched. 'You're a fan?' he asked, in surprise, and she found herself smiling into his enquiring face.

'I'm an owner,' she corrected him. 'I've got an old 750 back home.'

'No sweat!' The tension that had been between them as they'd walked up from the beach was suddenly lifted, and Joe led the way over to the powerful road machine with evident pride. 'Yeah,' he said, 'this is a fairly contemporary model. But I've got one of the old Ironheads back in Frisco.'

'An Ironhead!' Olivia was impressed. 'Oh, mine's just a fairly beaten-up Panhead with telescopic front forks. Big deal!'

'Hey, those old Glides, as we called them, were pretty impressive,' he declared energetically. 'Have you had it long? When did you get interested in bikes?'

'In Harleys,' Olivia corrected him lightly, running an admiring hand over the motorcycle's gleaming paintwork. 'Oh—well, I guess I've always been interested, but I bought my machine when I got the royalties from my first book.'

Joe grinned, their earlier contretemps forgotten. 'D'you want to ride it?' he asked. 'I can see the yearning in your eyes.' He swung the bike off its stand, and tested its balance. 'There you go. If you follow that path through the trees, it'll bring you down to the beach.'

'Oh, no.' Olivia stepped back, shaking her head, one hand moving negatively from side to side. 'Really, I couldn't,' she added ruefully. 'Besides—the sand will get into the engine. It's kind of you to offer, but—'

'These bikes race on the beach at Daytona,' said Joe drily. 'But, if you're nervous of having a skid, hop on the back.' He patted the seat, and although Olivia knew it was reckless she found herself doing as he suggested, and a moment later he had started the powerful machine and pulled away.

'Hold on,' he yelled as they started down a tree-lined track that was narrow and undoubtedly dangerous for an unskilled rider, although Olivia felt no fear with Joe in charge. With a feeling of excitement, she slipped her arms about his waist and hung on tightly, revelling equally in the thrill of the ride and the nearness of his taut frame.

Once they reached the beach, he opened it up, and they sped along the damp sand so fast that the barrette came out of Olivia's hair and blew away. But it was so exhilarating to feel the wind tearing at her scalp that she hardly noticed. She'd never ridden without a helmet before.

He turned at speed, the rear wheel sliding madly across the sand, and then he brought the powerful engine to a halt. 'Your turn,' he said, getting off the bike, and this time she didn't object.

She didn't drive as fast as Joe. She wasn't used to having a pillion rider, for one thing, and for another she was intensely conscious of Joe's hands at her waist. He didn't cling to her, but he did grasp a handful of her hair and wrap it round his fingers. 'It's blinding me,' he said, into her ear, and the bike wobbled as Olivia felt his hand against her neck.

She stopped again before the path started up to the house. 'You take over now,' she said, her cheeks scarlet from the wind.

'Okay.' He slid across the seat, and grasped the handlebars. 'You did good,' he added admiringly, and Olivia scrambled onto the back to hide her foolish pride.

They reached the patio all too soon, and when Joe parked the bike in its previous position Olivia was ready to swing her leg to the ground. 'Wait.' His hand gripped her bare leg just above her knee, successfully stopping her. He turned and looked at her over his shoulder, his eyes warmly sensual as they rested on her flushed face. 'I just wanted you to know I'm—sorry about what happened before—'

'It doesn't matter—'

'It does.' His fingers splayed over her knee. 'It wasn't your fault, it was mine.'

Olivia's knee quivered beneath his fingers, and to distract him from that stark betrayal she uttered a forced laugh. 'You can tell I've spent too long at a desk. I'm out of condition,' she said, hoping he'd believe her. But all he did was slide his hand up her thigh, his fingers invading the hem of her shorts.

'I can tell when you're lying,' he said softly, and dampness pooled between her legs. God, could he smell the effect his words were having on her? Every pore in her body was oozing sexual need.

'I've got to go,' she said desperately, and abruptly he released her.

'Yeah, I know,' he muttered harshly as she fairly vaulted off the bike. 'But I want you to know I'm glad you came here. And I hope you'll want to see me again...'

Olivia dragged her thoughts back to the present. He'd not meant it, she assured herself. He was just being polite, letting her off the hook for taking advantage of the situation earlier on. He hadn't wanted to send her back to the hotel thinking that what had happened had disturbed him. He'd probably been trying to ensure that she didn't spill the beans to Diane.

As if she would!

Olivia sighed. She would say nothing to Diane. Apart from anything else, telling tales would require her to admit that she'd been at the Malibu house, and that was something she'd rather keep to herself. Stupid as it was, she preferred to keep the memory private. It had been an afternoon out of time, a few hours when she'd had him all to herself.

All the same, Diane's question demanded an answer, and she'd spent far too long staring into space. 'Yesterday afternoon?' she repeated lightly, as if it were difficult to remember. 'Why? Were you trying to reach me?' She manufactured an enquiring look. 'I—went shopping.'

'Did you?' Diane's response was ominous, but Olivia assured herself she couldn't possibly know what she'd really done. Unless someone had seen B.J. when he'd come to collect her. Despite Joe's protests, she'd insisted on coming back in a cab. 'I was trying to reach you,' Diane added coolly, crossing one silk-clad leg over the other. 'Joe was too busy to see me, and I wanted to talk about the book.'

'Really?'

Olivia bent her head and set her coffee cup carefully back on its saucer. She had the uneasy feeling that nothing about this morning was usual at all. First the coffee, and now this interrogation. Diane had never shown an interest in what she'd done before.

'Yes, really,' said Diane now, leaning towards her. Her blue eyes were steely sharp in her delicate face. 'I think you'll agree that we've covered most of the personal details. It occurred to me that you'd probably rather not discuss your husband's attraction to me. Like the details about my other two marriages, I'm sure Phoebe can give you what you need. And, of course, you'll want to visit the studios. She can arrange that, too.'

Olivia cleared her throat. 'I see,' she said, and caught her lower lip between her teeth. 'Then you don't want me coming here again—on a regular basis, that is?'

Diane seemed to hesitate, and Olivia steeled herself for some outburst, but then the other woman merely shook her head. 'No,' she said, picking a thread of cotton from her short linen tunic. 'It's too—boring. I've got things to do, people to see, appointments to keep. Spending every morning closeted with you is much too demanding. I'm neglecting my—friends, and—Joe's complaining because I'm never free.'

Olivia stiffened. Had that been deliberate? She was almost sure it had. 'I'm sorry you find talking about yourself boring,' she said tightly, and then cursed herself for letting her feelings show.

'I didn't say that,' retorted Diane. 'I said spending every morning with you was boring. God, I don't know what Ricky sees in you. What he ever saw, if it comes to that.'

Olivia got to her feet. 'In that case—' she began, feeling an intense sense of relief that it was all over, but before she could move away Diane uttered a remorseful sound.

'Oh, please,' she said, getting up now and offering her famous smile in conciliation. 'I'm so sorry, Olivia. That was unforgivable. But Ricky gets me so on edge at times I don't know what I'm doing. Really, that wasn't what I intended to say at all.'

But it was what she was thinking, thought Diane uneasily, not at all convinced that her ex-husband was the only reason for this scene. 'I think we both know that my coming here was a mistake,' she declared swiftly. 'I'm sorry if Richard's making life difficult for you, but—'

'No. Please.' Diane's smile had thinned now, and Olivia knew it wasn't only her imagination that made her think that it didn't reach her eyes. 'Sit down, Olivia. Let me explain.'

'There's nothing to explain—'

'There is.' Diane's tone was still polite, but Olivia had the feeling she was only keeping her temper with an effort.

'I suppose the truth is I didn't realise it would—upset Ricky so much. Having you here, I mean.'

'Ms Haran—'

'No, let me finish.' Diane sank down onto the sofa again, and rather than continue standing over her Olivia felt compelled to resume her seat. 'I—told Ricky I wouldn't say anything; that I'd pretend this was my idea and not his. But, you're obviously far too intelligent to be put off with half-truths, when you probably know how he feels for yourself.'

Olivia sighed. 'I don't think—'

'Hear me out, please.' Diane put out an imploring hand. 'I've spoken to Phoebe, and she agrees with me. You can get anything you need from her. You can stay on at the hotel, of course—until the end of the week, at least. Then send me the first draft of the manuscript when it's completed. I can fax any amendments I think are necessary.'

'But I thought—'

The words were out before she could prevent them, and Olivia knew a feeling of frustration when Diane lifted one expertly plucked brow. 'You thought?' she said, evidently prepared to listen in this instance. Had she guessed what Olivia had been thinking? 'Go on. What were you about to say?'

'It was nothing,' said Olivia firmly, annoyed with herself for saying anything. She had no intention of admitting that she'd been looking forward to writing the first draft of the book in Los Angeles. 'I—if you're still sure you want me to write your biography—'

'I do.'

'Then—okay. I can do that.'

'Good.' Diane nodded. 'Good.' She paused. 'I'll tell Ricky you're leaving.'

'Oh, please—' Now it was Olivia's turn to make an imploring gesture. 'I'd rather you didn't say anything.' She felt the annoying heat of her embarrassment entering her cheeks. She wanted no more roses arriving at the hotel. 'I—I think it's best, don't you?'

'If you say so.' But Diane's face had a strangely feral look to it now, and Olivia wondered if she had been entirely wise to show her feelings. 'But now I suggest you finish your coffee, and then we'll try and tie up any loose ends you feel are still outstanding.'

CHAPTER TWELVE

OLIVIA sighed, sinking lower into the foaming water and allowing the powerful jets to ease her cares away. This was a luxury she wouldn't have when she got back to England, and although it was something she could live without it was just another reminder that this time tomorrow night she'd be on the plane to London.

She sighed again, putting up her hand to check that her hair was still secured in the knot she'd pinned earlier. Wet strands clung to her cheeks, but she was relieved to find the knot was holding. She didn't have time to wash her hair tonight. Not if she wanted to get down to the restaurant at a reasonable hour.

Of course, she was late because Max Audrey, Diane's producer, had kept her waiting so long at the studios. Like a few of the people she'd contacted in the past few days, he considered his job far more important than hers. She wasn't rich, therefore she was expendable. In his world only money oiled the wheels of success.

And when she'd finally got to talk to him he'd been less than courteous. His phone had kept ringing throughout the interview, and he hadn't asked her to excuse him every time he'd reached for the receiver. She had the feeling she could have learned as much about his opinion of Diane if she'd spoken to his secretary. Just as Manuel and María knew their employer better than anyone else.

Still, she had learned a lot more about her subject's standing in the film community. Phoebe had arranged for her to visit the studios where Diane's last film had been made, and Olivia had spoken to cameramen and technicians, make-up artists, and her director, all of whom had been generous in the anecdotes they'd conveyed. Apparently, Diane was well liked by the people who'd

142

worked with her, but Olivia couldn't help the suspicion that they'd have said anything to keep their jobs.

It had been a strenuous week, made more so by the fact that she'd been constantly in Phoebe's presence. Diane's agent had insisted that it would be easier for her if she came along. Once again, Olivia suspected that her motives weren't all altruistic. She had the feeling Diane had sent her to ensure she didn't spend her time with anyone else.

As if...

Olivia's lips tightened a little at the realisation that it was almost a week since she'd spent that afternoon with Joe. She hadn't really expected him to get in touch with her again, but she couldn't help feeling disappointed that she hadn't even seen him about the hotel. He'd probably gone back to San Francisco and thought nothing more about her, she reflected ruefully. Except, perhaps, a sense of relief that he'd avoided a more disastrous scene.

The realisation that the phone was ringing jarred her out of her introspection. Diane, she thought wearily. She often rang at this time. To check up on her? Olivia was cynical. If she only knew, she had nothing to check up on her for. But if she didn't answer the phone Diane would be suspicious, and the last thing she wanted was for her to come to the hotel.

Switching off the jets, she sat up and reached for the extension. Like all the best establishments, there was a phone in the bathroom as well. It had been a novelty when she'd first got here, but pretty soon the novelty had worn off. It meant there was no place where Diane couldn't reach her, which was one advantage she would have when she went home.

Her hand slipped on the receiver and she almost dropped it into the bath so that there was a lilt of laughter in her voice when she said, 'Hello.' And why not? she thought determinedly. She should be looking forward to seeing her flat again. And Henry! She pulled a wry face. She hoped he hadn't forgotten all about her.

'Liv?'

Her heart sank. 'Hello, Richard,' she said, wishing she hadn't answered after all.

'Liv, I want to see you. Diane says that you're leaving, and I must talk to you before you go. I know it's late, and you're probably exhausted, but I can't let you go without making you understand how I feel.'

'No, Richard.'

'What do you mean, no?'

'I mean I don't want to see you,' said Olivia flatly. 'I'm sorry, but that's the way it is. I—I'm sure you and Diane can iron your problems out if you just put your minds to it.' She paused. 'Have you thought of having a baby? If I remember correctly that was one of the reasons why you wanted a divorce.'

'Oh, yes.' Richard sneered. 'You had to bring that up, didn't you? You know as well as I do that I can't father a child.'

'I didn't know that,' protested Olivia, dry-mouthed, as the injustice of his accusations assailed her. She swallowed. 'But thank you for telling me.' She shook her head. 'Better late than never.'

Richard swore. 'Are you trying to tell me you didn't have any suspicions that I was to blame?'

'No, I didn't.' Olivia caught her breath. 'How could I? You swore it wasn't you.'

'I swore a lot of things,' muttered Richard bitterly. 'But you didn't hear them all. I can't believe you didn't check up on me. After I'd left, at least.'

'And they'd have told me?' Olivia was impatient. 'Get real, Richard. A person's medical history is private. Besides—' she drew a trembling breath '—I had no reason to believe you were lying.'

'No.' He sounded frustrated now. 'I guess I have been a complete bastard!' He sighed. 'That's why I want you to forgive me. You've no idea how much your—understanding would mean to me.'

Olivia bit her lip. 'All right,' she said. 'All right, I forgive you. Now—I've got to go. I'm—busy, and I want to get on.'

'Still working?' Richard was sardonic. 'My, what a conscientious little girl you are.' And then, as if sensing her indignation, he added, 'Sorry. That was uncalled for.' He paused. 'Maybe I'll speak to you again before you leave.'

Not if I have anything to do with it, thought Olivia fiercely as she replaced the receiver. She could only hope Diane hadn't told him exactly when she was leaving. But, as she'd told him everything else, what chance did she have of that?

The phone rang again, almost before she'd had time to settle down again. The final few moments she'd been promising herself were obviously not meant to be. 'Yes?' she said ungraciously, wondering what else Richard could have thought of, and then almost lost her voice when Joe Castellano's husky tenor caressed her ear.

'Olivia? Hi.' He paused. 'I was wondering. Have you had dinner?'

Olivia collapsed against the side of the bath. 'Joe,' she said, when she could speak again. Her voice was strangely hoarse. 'What a surprise.'

'But a pleasant one, I hope,' he said, though there was an unexpected edge to his voice. 'I—don't want to intrude on your privacy, but I'd like to see you. If you haven't had dinner, perhaps we could eat together.'

Olivia expelled a trembling breath. 'I—haven't had dinner,' she said, realising she didn't sound very enthusiastic, but too overwhelmed by his sudden phone call to select her words.

'Well, good.' He waited a beat. 'Does that mean you do want to see me? Or was that merely an observation, and you'd rather eat alone?'

'No, I—' Olivia struggled to pull herself together. 'You don't understand. Um—Richard was on the phone just now, and I thought it was him calling back.' She moistened her lips, and then forced herself to continue. 'I—suppose I thought you'd be dining with Diane.'

'Well, I'm not.' He didn't elaborate, so she didn't know whether that was her decision or his. 'Look, if you've made some arrangement to meet Richard, forget it. I should have given you some warning, but I just got back from Frisco this evening.'

So he had been away again.

Olivia hurried into speech. 'No, I'm not seeing Richard. And—and I'd love to have dinner with you. If—if you'll give me a few minutes, I'll be ready.'

'May I come up?'

Olivia's breathing was suspended. 'Come up?'

'Yeah, as in you offering me a drink before dinner,' he responded lightly. 'But if you'd rather not—'

'No.' Olivia gulped for air, and dismissed the thought that it wasn't a good idea. 'Please—' Her voice cracked, and she cleared her throat to hide her embarrassment. 'Yes. Come on up. I'll leave the door unlocked.'

Which meant wedging the 'Do Not Disturb' notice between the door and the lock, she discovered moments later, after flinging on one of the towelling bathrobes the hotel supplied and scurrying through the bedroom and across the sitting room in her bare feet. But if she'd told Joe she was still in the bath he might have suspected her of making excuses, and this might be her last chance of saying goodbye.

She had barely made it into the bath again before she heard someone enter the suite. She prayed it wasn't a prowler, and listened attentively to him closing the door. Then, 'Olivia?' she heard him call, and her breath escaped her in a relieved sigh.

'I'm here,' she called back lightly, and reached for the soap.

She was lathering her arms with one of the expensively perfumed cushions that appeared in various parts of the bathroom every morning and disappeared as soon as she had used them, when he opened the bathroom door. If he was surprised to find her in the bath he didn't show it.

Instead, he propped his shoulder against the frame of the door and regarded her as if he had every right to be there.

'Hi.'

Olivia was too shocked to speak, so she didn't say anything. She was too busy reviewing her Victorian morals, and finding them wanting. She was a modern woman, she chided herself, and it wasn't as if she wasn't attracted to him. But she'd never dreamt he might walk into the bathroom.

Her initial impulse was to slide down so that her body was hidden beneath the water. Her breasts were responding to his appraisal and their rosy peaks were already button-hard and tight. But he'd seen her breasts, she reminded herself, so surely they were no novelty to him, and he was not to know there was a pulse beating between her legs.

And he looked so good, she thought avidly, feeding on his dark attractive face. In a dark grey lounge suit and matching shirt, the jacket parted by the hand he'd pushed into his trouser pocket, he made her acutely aware of what she was missing by not having a man in her life.

She wouldn't have been human if she hadn't reacted, but instead of acting like a shrinking violet she continued soaping her arms as if having a man standing watching her were an everyday occurrence. She wasn't aware of being deliberately provocative, even when her hands strayed to her breasts, but his sudden instinctive intake of breath brought a half-challenging look to her eyes.

'D'you want some help?' he asked huskily, and now she was forced to look away. But she wondered what he was doing here when a week ago he'd made his feelings blatantly obvious.

'I don't think so,' she said, finding her voice at last. 'If—if you'll help yourself to a drink, I'll be with you as soon as I can.'

'I don't want a drink,' he countered, and, straightening away from the door, he approached the huge corner bath. His eyes darkened as they looked down at her. 'Is there room for another one in there?'

Olivia's jaw sagged. 'I—why—no—'

'Why not?' He squatted down on his haunches beside her. 'My architect informed me that these tubs are big enough to hold a party.'

'Well, they're not.' Olivia was swift to disabuse him, the idea of provoking him again losing its appeal. 'Besides—' she forced herself to meet his sensual gaze '—I thought you weren't interested in me.'

His eyes narrowed. 'What gave you that idea?'

'What gave me that idea?' echoed Olivia disbelievingly. 'I should have thought you'd know that better than me.'

'Well, I don't,' he said annoyingly, dipping his hand into the water and allowing its contents to spill over her shoulder and down her breast. 'In any case, I thought this was what you wanted. If not, you did a damn good job of convincing me that it was.'

Olivia swallowed, his nearness overwhelming the urge to send him away. And though she doubted her motives had anything do to with Richard what he was suggesting was temptation in its finest form.

But she couldn't do this, she thought unsteadily. He'd said she was no *femme fatale* and he was right. And in her prescribed world people didn't act so recklessly. She trembled at the thought of him getting into the bath with her. God, she could imagine her father's reaction if he could see her now.

Taking a deep breath, she turned to look at him. 'What do you really want?' she asked, uncaring if he thought her naïve.

Instead of answering her, however, he picked up the soap and lathered his hands with it. 'Isn't it obvious?' he asked, and stroked his hand down her cheek.

'Not to me,' she lied, even though her heart was thumping. Dear God, did he really mean precisely what he said? 'You're wetting your sleeve,' she added, hoping to distract him. His cuff had trailed in the water and was dripping on her arm.

'So what?' he asked now, but he rinsed his hands and

shed his jacket onto the floor. 'That better?' he suggested, his gaze moving deliberately over her body, and she pressed her thighs together almost in defence.

'Mr Castellano—'

He was pulling off his tie and loosening his collar as she said this, and he rested his forearms on the bath and gave her a knowing look. 'Don't call me that, for God's sake,' he said drily. 'This isn't the 1890s. I don't make love to women who call me Mr Castellano.'

'Then perhaps that's what I should call you, Mr Castellano,' responded Olivia breathily, aware that it was his teasing that was making her feel brave.

'Could be,' he agreed smoothly, disconcerting her. He slipped off his shirt and unbuttoned the waistband of his trousers. 'I can always make an exception in your case.'

Olivia's eyes widened. 'Joe—' she gasped in protest. 'You can't do this.'

But he'd pushed himself to his feet and was already tackling his zip. 'You can help me,' he said, kicking off his loafers and stepping out of his trousers. And as she looked up at him in mute confusion he added, pointing at his silk boxers, 'You can tell me if you want me to keep these on for modesty's sake.'

Olivia couldn't answer him. She'd never been in a situation like this before and he took her tightened lips as her assent. Before she could move aside, he had stepped down into the deep water, his legs brushing hers as he sat down opposite.

Although she knew she should look elsewhere, she found herself staring at him. Was this some crazy dream, or was Joe Castellano actually sharing her bath? She moved her foot and her toes brushed a hair-roughened calf and ankle. It was really him, and she flinched at the contact.

'Isn't this cosy?' he said, spreading his arms along the sides of the bath and relaxing completely. He took a breath. 'Don't tell me you've never done anything like this before.'

'I haven't,' said Olivia tersely, wishing she was more

experienced. Her eyes felt riveted to the dark hair beneath his arms.

And not just beneath his arms, she noticed. She could now see the hair that arrowed down below his waist. Richard's skin had been smooth, she remembered, and it had always been a source of annoyance to him. But Olivia had always told him she didn't like hairy men.

And she didn't, she insisted fiercely, wishing she could just ignore him. But she couldn't make a move without encountering his outstretched feet. And just when she thought he couldn't do anything more to upset her he drew up his knees and moved so that her feet were between his legs.

'What do you—?' she began unsteadily, and then broke off when he grasped her ankles. 'What do you think you're doing?' she finished breathlessly as his hands slid over her slim calves.

'I thought you might like a massage,' he responded, without looking at her. He was looking down at his hands, at what they were doing to her legs. 'I'm good at this sort of thing,' he added huskily, moving closer until her toes were brushing his groin.

Olivia's stomach quivered. She could feel the swollen heat of him against her feet, and although she knew it was crazy she wished he wasn't wearing the boxers after all. There was something intensely intimate about touching him in this way.

'Like it?' he asked, looking up at her through his straight lashes, and Olivia, who had been scarcely aware of his kneading fingers, could only nod her head. 'I told you I was good,' he appended softly. 'Come closer and I'll loosen up your thighs.'

Olivia's breath escaped in a sound that was half-gulp, half-sob, and she wondered if he could hear the hysteria in her voice. If he only knew, she thought, suppressing the urge to tell him. If he loosened her up any more she'd fall apart.

Yet she didn't stop him when he moved even closer, and

she was obliged to draw her knees up to her chest. 'Open your legs,' he directed roughly, and she heard the raw emotion underlying the request. His thumb brushed over her lower lip. 'Open your mouth.'

Olivia's legs slid down, under his, and he parted his knees and moved closer still. They were face to face and limb to limb, his chest hair tickling her breasts, their lower bodies barely inches apart.

'You're the sexiest woman I've ever known, do you know that?' he muttered, his tongue stroking her lips. He gripped her waist and brought her closer, his thumbs caressing the underside of her breasts.

Sexy? Her?

Olivia felt dizzy, as much from what he was saying as from the tantalising touch of his mouth. But between her legs his arousal was hard against her softness, pushing with urgent need against his shorts.

'You don't mean that,' she said unsteadily, when he released her mouth to nuzzle the hollow of her neck.

'Don't I?' He bit her deliberately, sucking the soft flesh into his mouth 'I'm not—Richard,' he added, when he was able to speak again. 'I don't say things I don't mean.'

Olivia expelled a tremulous breath. 'I don't want to talk about Richard right now.'

'And nor do I,' he conceded, his hands moving up to encircle her breasts. His thumbs pressed almost cruelly on her taut nipples. 'But I want you to know I'm not him.'

'I—I'm not likely to forget,' she got out jerkily, her own hands coming up to grip his waist. And although she wondered later how she'd found the courage to do it her fingers slid inside the waistband of his shorts.

'God...'

His involuntary recoil was instantaneous as her slim fingers explored his buttocks, and for one awful moment she thought he was going to vault out of the bath. She closed her eyes for a moment, not sure she could bear it if he did so, but when she opened them again he was peeling the boxers off his legs. He tossed them aside without taking his eyes from her, and she felt her limbs melting beneath his sensual gaze. 'Come here,' he muttered huskily, reclaiming his position, and this time she felt his muscled heat between her legs.

There was no barrier between them now, no film of silk to prevent an intimacy she'd never known before. When his hand slipped down between them to find the aching nub that craved his attention, she arched helplessly against his fingers, unable to hold back.

Wave upon wave of feeling swept over her, and she sought his mouth eagerly, thrusting her tongue between his teeth. Her hands were gripping his neck, holding him even closer, and he groaned deep in his throat at this evidence of how sweetly responsive she really was.

'Easy, now,' he said unsteadily as she covered his face with kisses, but he turned his mouth against hers with increasing need. His fingers were in her now, stroking her slick honeycomb, making her feel as if she was drowning in sensual pleasure.

But she was instantly aware of the moment when his male sex replaced his fingers. His muscled hardness spread the petals that enfolded him, thick and heavy, thrusting into her core. But her body deepened, expanded, stretched to meet his need, until they were closer than ever before.

'Am I hurting you?' he asked harshly as he heard her sudden intake of breath, but she shook her head and wound her arms around his neck.

'It feels—perfect,' she said huskily, curling her legs about him. She caressed his ear with her tongue. 'Is it good for you?'

Joe gave a groan. 'It's good,' he assured her thickly, closing his eyes. 'But God knows how long I can stand this. I have the feeling that if you move I'll spill my guts.'

'Not your guts, surely,' murmured Olivia breathlessly, never having shared her feelings with anyone else. Richard had been adequate, but not romantic; not adventurous at all. She rocked against Joe deliberately. 'D'you mean like that?'

He swore then, but it wasn't an angry sound, though she glimpsed the undisguised anguish in his face. 'If you want this to be over, just go on the way you are,' he told her, suppressing a moan. 'Oh, God, I don't think I want to wait any longer.'

It took only a moment. Pressing her against the bath, he withdrew only a couple of times before his thrusting body shuddered in her arms. And she found to her amazement that her own climax followed his, the tremors of his ejaculation and the spilling warmth of his seed driving her over the brink...

CHAPTER THIRTEEN

HE TOOK her again later, on the carelessly tumbled covers of her bed. Somehow, he found the strength to lift her out of the water and carry her into her bedroom, and, uncaring that they were wet, he sought a second release.

Then he rolled groaning onto his back, gathering her against him with lazy arms. 'You are beautiful,' he told her urgently, his hand cupping her breast. 'Richard must have been crazy to let you go.'

Olivia propped herself up on one elbow. 'I've told you,' she said tensely. 'I don't want to talk about Richard.' But when she looked at Joe she found he'd closed his eyes.

'Okay, okay,' he conceded drowsily. 'God, but I'm exhausted! Can we leave it till I've had some sleep?'

'Leave what?' she persisted, wanting him to commit himself, but Joe's breathing warned her he wasn't listening to her. He was breathing deeply, his dark lashes spread against his tanned face giving him a curious vulnerability, his impressive manhood dormant now in its moist nest of curling dark hair.

'Damn,' she muttered, barely audibly, taking a deep breath and sliding off the bed. He offered an involuntary movement of protest, but he was too far gone to waken, and she took the quilt and flung it over his sleeping form.

In the living room, the undrawn curtains displayed an unreal vista of downtown Los Angeles. As she tied the belt of her robe about her, she saw the ribbons of incandescence marking every street and highway, a multicoloured panorama of fairy lights. Every now and then, the solid bulk of a tall building added its own illumination to the scene. So many lights, she thought; so many people. Were any of them feeling as confused and anxious as she was tonight?

What to do?

She glanced back at the bedroom. Joe was obviously exhausted. He would probably sleep for several hours. But she had a distinct feeling of hollowness inside. She told herself it was hunger; that she'd feel better if she had some dinner. But she suspected its origins were far more complicated than that.

What was she going to do? What would he—Joe—expect her to do? He hadn't mentioned anything about her leaving the following day, but that didn't mean he didn't know she was going. If he was as intimate with Diane as Richard would have her believe, surely she'd have mentioned the change of plan to him?

Diane!

Olivia shivered. She'd almost forgotten Diane's part in this during the last couple of hours. But she'd certainly had her revenge, if that was what she'd been looking for, so why did she feel as if it was herself that she'd betrayed?

She shook her head. The answer was too painful to consider right now. She didn't want to think about the possibility that Joe might eventually marry Diane. How ignorant she'd been to imagine that what she'd felt for Richard was all there was to feel.

A feeling of nausea rose into the back of her throat but she fought it down. She was hungry, she told herself again. Once she'd got some food inside her, she'd stop feeling as if the bottom had dropped out of her world. She didn't love Joe Castellano. She couldn't. She was letting the sexual pleasure he'd given her blind her to his faults.

And he'd never said he cared about her. Not once. He'd told her that she was sexy, and beautiful—both attributes unwarranted, she was sure. But he'd never said he loved her, or that he wanted to spend the rest of his life with her. Heaven knew, he hadn't even mentioned that he wanted to see her again.

She shivered again. She should have told him she was leaving. Before she'd invited him up to the suite, she should have made it known that it was for a farewell drink. That way, he wouldn't have got the wrong impression—that she had intended that he should find her in the bath. As it was, he'd assumed her actions were a form of provocation. That when she'd unlocked the door, and answered his greeting, she'd been deliberately inciting his response.

Even so, she sighed, she couldn't have anticipated what would happen. Even in her wildest dreams, she'd never have imagined that he might join her in the bath. Dear God, in all the time she'd been married to Richard, he'd never done anything so outrageous. Or exciting, she admitted incredulously. Every nerve in her body quivered with expectancy when she remembered how desirable he'd made her feel.

She strayed to the open bedroom door again, but Joe was still sleeping. He'd rolled onto his stomach in her absence and his face was buried in the pillow where her head had been. She badly wanted to go in there and wake him and ask him what he intended. But what stopped her was the thought that he might tell her.

She felt the hollowness again, and this time her stomach rumbled. Perhaps it would be a good idea to go and get something to eat. She thought of calling Room Service, but in that case she'd feel obliged to order for two. And the last thing she wanted on her bill was proof that she'd been sharing her suite with someone else.

But what if Joe woke up and found she wasn't there? she fretted. If she left him a note, he could always come and join her downstairs. She sighed. Wouldn't a note be rather presumptuous? she argued worriedly. He might not want to join her for dinner now. The situation had changed.

For the better?

She wasn't certain. Richard had said he had proof that Diane and Joe were having an affair, so what was this all about? Was she perhaps just a brief diversion? If he knew she was leaving tomorrow, he must know there was no future in it.

With a feeling of despair, she went back into the bathroom and took a shower. Then, as he still hadn't stirred, she donned a silk bra and panties, and a sleeveless dress that fell to her ankles. Her hair was still damp, so she plaited it into a thick braid and secured it with a ribbon. Then, without even looking back, she left the room.

Downstairs, the hotel was busy. She didn't try to get a reservation for dinner in the Pineapple Room this evening, choosing the Bistro instead, for reasons best known to herself. She refused to acknowledge she'd chosen the Italian restaurant because of Joe's background, but she couldn't forget that he'd been eating in here the night she'd decided to play the vamp.

And, although she ordered her favourite pasta dish, she found she couldn't eat it. She was pushing it desultorily round her plate, when someone came to cast a shadow across the meal. She looked up in sudden relief, convinced it must be Joe come to find her. But it was a woman, and her heart sagged with disappointment.

'Hello, Miss Pyatt. Remember me?'

She was vaguely familiar, and Olivia was racking her brains, trying to think where she'd seen her before, when she saw the copy of Eileen Cusack's biography tucked under her arm. 'Oh, yes,' she said, somewhat flatly. 'You're the woman who thought I was Elizabeth Jennings.'

'Sherie Madsen,' supplied the woman eagerly. 'Yes, that's right.' She paused, as if she needed time to formulate what she was about to say. 'Um—did you get the roses?'

Olivia blinked. 'You sent the roses?'

'Well, it was my husband, actually,' Sherie admitted ruefully. 'After the patience you showed over my mistake, he said it was the least we could do.'

'Well, thank you.' Olivia was stunned. She'd never have suspected these people. 'And—and yes. They were beautiful. Thank you very much.'

'It's our pleasure.'

A man spoke, and Olivia saw Sherie's husband behind her now. He was smiling, too, and despite her disappointment Olivia couldn't help feeling flattered.

'Anyway, I just—well, I wondered if you'd mind signing your book now,' Sherie continued, proffering the biography. 'I haven't read it yet, but I'm taking it home to Wisconsin and I assure you I will.'

Olivia smiled. 'Not at all.' She held out her hand for the book and Sherie's husband quickly handed her a pen. She made the dedication and signed her name, and then gave it back to her admirer. 'I hope you enjoy it,' she added as they bid her goodnight.

The unexpected experience had lifted her spirits somewhat, so that by the time she went back up to her suite she was feeling slightly more optimistic than before. She closed the door with some care, and hurried to the door of the bedroom. But, although she'd been away less than an hour, Joe was gone.

The flight to Heathrow left at six o'clock and Olivia, who had been hanging around the airport since just after four, knew a curious kind of relief when the plane lifted off the ground. The decision was made, she thought. She was leaving. Whatever misgivings she might have had that morning were all behind her now. She'd checked out of the hotel, and she was on her way to London. The sooner she reached home and resumed a normal existence, the sooner she'd be able to put all thoughts of Joe Castellano out of her mind.

Well, that was what she'd told herself, she reflected ruefully as the big jet banked over the sprawling city below. She'd come here reluctantly, and she was going home in like mind. The only difference was the reasons. She'd exchanged one unhappy association for another.

But, despite her reluctance to leave Los Angeles, she was glad the past twenty-four hours were over. Making love—or, more accurately, having sex, she amended bitterly—with Joe had been exciting, she had to admit, but it was what had come after that had destroyed what little faith she'd had in herself. How could he do it? she wondered. How could he make love to her and then leave her, without even bothering to say farewell? When she'd got back to the suite and found he'd gone, it had been one of the worst moments of her life.

Yet, even then, she hadn't quite believed it. She'd been quite prepared to accept that Joe had woken up in her absence and gone to look for her. In consequence she'd gone back down to the lobby, only to have no success in any of the restaurants or bars. He wasn't even enjoying an espresso in the coffee shop, despite the fact that neither of them had had anything to eat.

She'd gone back to the suite, half hoping he might have turned up there; but he hadn't, and although she'd contemplated contacting Reception she hadn't been convinced he'd appreciate her doing that. The trouble was, she hadn't known what her position was as far as he was concerned, and the last thing she wanted to do was embarrass him—or herself, which was much more likely.

Realising she'd never sleep unless she had something to eat, she'd ordered a sandwich from Room Service, and forced herself to eat it when it arrived. Then, because she had to do something, she'd rung the phone company and asked if they could give her the number of the house at Malibu.

Of course, they couldn't. It was what they called an 'unpublished' number, and once again she'd come up against a brick wall. Short of alerting all his staff she was looking for him, she'd been helpless, and, deciding she would think of something else in the morning, she'd gone to bed.

She hadn't slept very well. Although she was physically tired, her brain refused to rest, and by six o'clock she'd been sitting at the window again. Why had he left? she'd asked herself, for what must have been the umpteenth time. If there'd been some sort of emergency, surely he'd have let her know.

When the phone had rung at eight o'clock, she'd been sure it must be him, ringing to offer his apologies, but it was Bonnie Lovelace instead. She'd been ringing to remind her that the usual checkout time was noon. 'But Diane's had me extend that to four o'clock,' she'd added grandly. 'She also said to tell you that she'd have invited you to the house, but she's away right now.'

'Is she?'

Olivia hadn't been particularly interested in what Diane was doing, but Bonnie had adopted her usual self-important style. 'Yes, she left last night for Malibu,' she'd continued, as if she was bestowing a confidence. 'She's staying with Mr Castellano. She said to tell you goodbye.'

That was the moment when Olivia's world had fallen apart. How could he do it? she thought. How could he have gone from her bed to Diane's? Or invite her to *his* bed, she amended, suppressing a moan of anguish. Were all men such bastards, or did she just attract that kind?

The rest of the day had been an anticlimax. Although she'd gone down to the lobby to buy some last-minute presents, her heart hadn't been in it, and she couldn't wait for four o'clock to come. As it was, she'd left for the airport with almost an hour to spare, and spent the rest of her time in Los Angeles in the departure lounge.

Even then, even after all that had happened, she'd still nurtured the hope that she might be wrong. He would know what time she was leaving. He'd said himself he was a frequent traveller. But, although she'd listened intently to every announcement from the public-address system, there was never one for her.

So, it was over, she told herself painfully. She hadn't come here with the best of intentions, so perhaps it served her right. She'd wanted to hurt Diane, but all she'd ended up doing was hurting herself. Which was probably nothing more than she deserved.

The plane had levelled off now, and the warning sign about fastening your seat belt had been switched off. The pilot had introduced himself by way of the microphones above her head, and he was presently telling his passengers what kind of flight they might expect. The forecast, he said, was good, and with a tail wind they should make good time. He expected to land the plane in London at twelve o'clock the following afternoon.

'Is this seat taken?'

Olivia, who had been grateful that the seat beside her

was unoccupied, looked up in surprise. To her dismay, she found Richard easing himself down beside her, his expression a mixture of satisfaction and smug relief.

Her jaw dropped. 'What are you doing here?' she exclaimed, rather too loudly, and then, at his gesture of protest, she lowered her tone. 'I mean…' She glanced with some embarrassment at the stewardess who was watching them. 'Why are you on this flight?'

Richard leaned back in his seat. 'Why do you think?' he asked impatiently, waving at the stewardess. 'Scotch,' he said, when the woman approached him, then, glancing down at what Olivia was drinking, an amused smile crossed his face. 'White wine,' he remarked triumphantly. 'D'you want another one of those?'

'No, thank you.' Olivia controlled her temper with difficulty. This was not a good time for Richard to try and rekindle their relationship. 'I asked you what you were doing on this flight.'

'And I told you,' retorted Richard comfortably, settling more comfortably in his chair as the stewardess went to get his drink.

'No. You said, why did *I* think you were travelling,' Olivia corrected him tersely. 'And I really don't have an answer for that.'

Richard's mouth turned down. 'If you say so.'

'I do say so.' Olivia closed her eyes for a moment in an effort to keep her emotions in check. Then she opened them again and looked at him coldly. 'Where's your wife? Or is that a leading question?'

'You know where she is,' muttered Richard sulkily. 'Bonnie told you.' And then, when Olivia frowned, he gave a defensive shrug. 'I was there. When she made the call,' he explained offhandedly. 'She told you were travelling on this flight. And—' He thought for a moment' and appended firmly, 'I decided to keep you company.'

'To keep me company?' Olivia was appalled. The last thing she wanted was Richard doing anything for her.

'Well, I have relatives in London, too,' he declared indignantly. 'It must be nine months since I saw my old man.'

'Really?' As Richard had seldom visited his father when he lived in England, that was hardly relevant. And she didn't believe that was his excuse for travelling now.

'Yes, really.' The stewardess brought his Scotch, and he took a moment to thank her before continuing. 'But I admit I took the chance to see you again. We couldn't talk before, what with Manuel listening in and so on. And that night in the bar you didn't give me a chance.'

'Oh, Richard...' Olivia spoke wearily now, wondering if she'd ever convince him she wasn't interested in him any more. 'We've said all we had to say. Whatever was between us is over. You're married to Diane, and I think you should give your marriage a second chance.'

'A second chance!' Richard sipped his Scotch derisively. 'Liv, I've told you Diane and I are washed up. Ever since Joe Castellano came on the scene, she's been running circles round herself trying to please him. I know he's invested a lot of money in her last two films, but that's not why she's been beating a path to his door.'

Olivia told herself she didn't want to hear this, but there was a strange kind of satisfaction in proving to herself that he'd been fooling her all along. 'You said—you said they were having an affair,' she murmured, trying to sound offhand, 'but how do you know that?' She moistened her lips. 'I read in a magazine that he was—seeing someone else.'

'Anna Fellini,' said Richard at once, evidently knowing all the details. 'Yeah, that's the woman his mother would have liked to welcome into the family.' He paused. 'It's the usual story: Giovanni Castellano—Joe's father—and Paolo Fellini were partners. Giovanni's dead now, but if Joe married Anna, her father would make his share of the vineyards over to him.'

Olivia expelled a low breath. 'I see.'

'But it's not going to happen,' continued Richard positively. 'Much as Castellano likes money, my guess is he likes Diane more.'

Olivia nodded. 'And—you've got proof?'

'Sure have.' Richard was smug. 'I've got a picture of them, together, in San Diego. And when I say together I mean *together*, if you get my drift.'

Olivia felt sick. 'You mean—?'

'Yeah. You got it. Naked, in bed; the whole nine yards.' His lips twisted. 'And Diane knows that picture is going to cost her. If she wants a divorce, she's got to make me happy first.'

Olivia stared at him. 'You wouldn't—'

'Wouldn't I?' Richard sneered. 'Don't you believe it. It was their mistake using that sleazy motel in the first place.' He chuckled, but it wasn't a pleasant sound. 'I heard her making the arrangements. That's how I was able to fix the pictures. I swear to God, you can get anything in L.A. if the price is right. She thought I was out, but I was listening on the extension in—in another room.'

He faltered over those last few words, and Olivia wondered what he had been about to say that he'd thought better of. Maybe the extension he'd been listening in on had been in someone else's room, she reflected sagely. Like Bonnie Lovelace's, for instance. Olivia knew she had rooms at the Beverly Hills mansion. And Richard had used that 'I swear to God' phrase again that Olivia had heard Bonnie use so many times before.

But this possible proof of Richard's duplicity didn't mean anything to her. It was what he'd said about Joe and Diane that made her feel sick at heart. She'd never have believed that Joe would leave himself open to any kind of extortion. And why use a motel in San Diego, when he owned a house in Malibu?

'I've shocked you, haven't I?' Richard said now, finishing his Scotch and ringing for the stewardess to order another. 'Well, don't worry. If there's any scandal, it won't reflect badly on me.'

'But have you told him?' asked Olivia, unable to prevent the automatic question. 'I mean, this is blackmail, isn't it? Isn't that a criminal offence?'

'I guess.' Richard was indifferent. 'But Diane's not going to let it get that far. It's her butt that's recognisable, not his.'

Olivia sucked in a breath. 'Are you saying it might not be—Joe Castellano, then?' she ventured faintly.

'Hell, no.' Richard was adamant. 'It's him all right. He used his own name when they checked in; can you believe it?' He snorted. 'Mr and *Mrs* Castellano! And Diane thinks I'm a dope.'

Olivia hesitated. 'Well—what if it's someone else using that name?' she suggested, and Richard's expression darkened as she spoke.

'Oh, yeah,' he said accusingly. 'You'd like to believe that. Don't think I don't know you had the hots for him yourself.'

Olivia gasped. 'I beg your pardon—?'

'Don't pretend you don't know what I'm talking about.' Richard's lips twisted. 'I saw you myself that afternoon at Malibu.' He smiled at her confusion, but there was no humour in it. 'Oh, yeah, I saw you tearing along the beach on the back of his Harley.'

Olivia was horrified. 'But—how—?'

'I was in the lobby of the hotel when that goon of his came to fetch you,' explained Richard carelessly. 'After the way you cut me up that morning, I knew there had to be a reason. So I staked out your hotel and bingo!—there he was.'

Olivia swallowed. 'I can't believe you'd do a thing like that!' she exclaimed, even as her mind was racing. She supposed she should be grateful he hadn't seen them at the house. She remembered thinking that the solarium was too exposed for lovemaking.

'Desperate needs take desperate measures,' he misquoted smugly. 'Diane was extremely interested to hear where you'd been.'

Olivia blinked. 'You told Diane?'

'Oh, yeah.' Richard picked up the glass the stewardess had just set beside him and viewed her over the rim.

'Why'd you think she changed her mind about you staying on at the hotel? If there's one thing Diane can't stand it's competition.'

Olivia couldn't believe it. 'You told Diane,' she said again. 'For God's sake, why?'

'Because I knew we weren't going to get it together in Lala-land,' he responded. 'And Castellano was a complication I couldn't afford.'

Olivia was stunned. 'I still can't believe you'd do this. Jeopardise your marriage and my career because you can't accept a simple truth. Richard, I told you, I don't love you, I don't care if I never see you again. You had no right to interfere in my life. No right at all.'

Richard's mouth took on a sullen slant. 'You're just saying that because you're angry with Diane. Once you've had time to think about it, I know you'll see I'm right. We were meant for one another, Liv, only I was too blind to see it before. And with the settlement Diane's promised me—'

'Richard, read my lips,' said Olivia grimly, staring at him. 'When we land in London, I never want to see you again. I'm sorry if you're not happy with Diane, but that's not my problem. Now, I suggest you go back to your own seat.'

Richard scowled. 'You don't mean that.'

'I do mean it.'

'You're wasting your time if you think Castellano will come after you,' Richard blurted suddenly. 'I told him you and I had decided to get back together, and that I was accompanying you home.'

'When?' Olivia gulped. 'When did you talk to Joe about our relationship?'

'Last night, of course,' said Richard sulkily. 'Where were you, by the way? When I phoned the suite the second time lover-boy answered the phone.'

CHAPTER FOURTEEN

JOE'S house was in Marin county, north of San Francisco. The houses here had magnificent views of the water, with the green hills surrounding the Berkeley campus visible across the bay. On a clear day, that was, the taxi driver had told Olivia cheerfully. The bay area could be foggy, especially in the height of summer. But it was always beautiful, he'd added proudly. Like all the locals she'd met so far, he never wanted to live anywhere else.

Which was probably why Joe lived here, too, she reflected tensely. That, and the fact that the vineyard he owned was in the Napa Valley, which wasn't far away.

Not that she wanted to think about the vineyard. To do so meant thinking about Anna Fellini, too, and she was one obstacle she was not yet prepared to face. For the present, it was enough to know that Joe wasn't with Diane. That her departure for Malibu had had nothing to do with him.

But that didn't mean she wasn't a fool for coming here, Olivia acknowledged. In fact, if she'd stopped to think what she was doing, she'd never have found the courage to book her flight. And, after all, she had no proof that Joe would want to see her. Only an instinct that was getting weaker by the minute.

Yet, when Richard had dropped his bombshell, she'd been determined to do something. Even if it was only speaking to Joe on the phone, and telling him what a liar her ex-husband was. It had seemed important that she should explain to him that it was not because of Richard that she was leaving. That she'd assumed he knew all about Diane's decision before he came to the hotel.

Getting rid of Richard at the airport hadn't been a problem. After she'd told him what she really thought of him, he'd barely spoken to her for the rest of the trip. He hadn't moved back to his own seat but she knew that was because he was too embarrassed to do so. He'd evidently told the stewardess they were old friends.

Friends!

Olivia had wanted to kill him. She'd told herself she should have suspected something was wrong when she got back to the suite and found Joe was gone. But the truth was, she'd had so little confidence in her own sexuality that, even though she'd tried to reach him by phone, she hadn't really believed he'd want to see her again.

Back at her flat, with Henry purring his welcome, she'd wondered what she could do. No one, least of all Diane and her cohorts, was going to give her Joe's number. She'd already faced that problem in L.A.

But that was when she'd thought of B.J. Benedict Jeremiah Freemantle. She was unlikely to forget his name. How many Benedict Jeremiah Freemantles were there likely to be in California? Although Joe's number had been unlisted, she couldn't believe B.J.'s would be as well.

And it wasn't. As she'd suspected, although his employer divided his time between Los Angeles and San Francisco, B.J.'s apartment was in L.A. He probably had a room at each of Joe's houses, too, just as Bonnie did at Diane's. But his own home was in Westwood, just like Phoebe's.

She'd rung B.J. later that same evening. But it was lunchtime in L.A. and all she'd got was his answering service. However, she'd been able to leave a message, asking him to call her, and she'd spent the next twenty-four hours praying that he would.

B.J. had eventually returned her call two days later. He'd been out of the city, he said, and he'd only just got back. He'd obviously been reluctant to tell her anything about his employer, but when Olivia had explained that it was a personal matter he'd seemed more suspicious than anything else.

It wasn't until Olivia had virtually revealed her feelings for Joe that he'd shown a little more interest. Joe wasn't still in L.A., he'd told her. He'd returned to San Francisco four nights ago. The same night he'd spoken to Richard, Olivia had realised numbly, wondering if she was a fool to pursue him like this.

But something had been driving her on, and somehow she'd succeeded in convincing B.J. that she had to speak to his employer again. But although he'd been prepared to give her Joe's address in San Francisco so she could write to him he had drawn the line at giving her his phone number.

And it was as she was putting down the phone that she had had this brainwave. The brainwave that had caused her to book herself a flight for the following day. She'd never been to San Francisco, she'd consoled herself as she'd paid her fare. If Joe refused to see her, she could always use the trip as research.

Not that that was a very convincing argument, she conceded now. She had the feeling that if Joe refused to speak to her she'd want to take the first flight home. She'd always preferred to lick her wounds in private, and her little flat had never seemed more appealing than it did right now.

'You sure this is the place you want?'

The taxi driver was looking at her reflection in the rear-view mirror, and Olivia guessed that with her cream cotton shirt, mud-brown skirt and bare legs she didn't look as if she'd be at home in these sprawling estates. Or perhaps he'd taken his cue from the small hotel where she was staying. She remembered now that he'd looked rather shocked when she'd given him the address.

'I'm sure,' she said, though her voice was constricted. Her nerves were tight enough without him voicing her own fears. Dear God, she must have been crazy coming here on the strength of a brief—if passionate—association. Would he even care that Richard hadn't been telling the truth?

A few minutes earlier, they'd left Highway 101 and the taxi was now descending a steep curve towards the water. Below them, she could see the roofs and main street of a small town. In the guidebook she'd bought at the airport, she'd read about Sausalito and Tiburon, and the ferry that plied across San Francisco Bay.

'Okay. Well, this is it,' the driver told her suddenly, and Olivia dragged her eyes from the hillside that fell away sharply on their left to the solid wooden gates that faced the road.

The roof of a house could be glimpsed between the trees that grew so thickly beyond the gates. Olivia could see turrets rising above the trees, and a cream-painted façade laced with wooden slats. It looked dignified and imposing, and nothing like the house at Malibu. Yet they each shared the quality of being unique in their own particular way.

And impressive, thought Olivia ruefully, avoiding the driver's eyes as she got out of the car. And how was she supposed to get inside? she wondered. As far as she could see, there was no bell or intercom in sight.

'D'you want me to hang around, in case no one's home?' The man took the dollars she'd offered him but he didn't immediately pull away.

'I— Oh, no.' Despite the distance she was from the nearest town, Olivia was loath to keep him hanging about. Besides, she thought, she could do without an audience if she was forced to abandon her trip.

'Okay.'

With some reluctance, the man put the vehicle into 'drive' and moved off down the road. He was probably hoping to pick up a fare down by the harbour, she decided, wondering if she'd made a huge mistake.

The sound of a car's horn almost scared the life out of her. While she had been fretting about the wisdom of letting the taxi go, a huge estate car had been bearing down on her, its flashing light indicating that it wanted to turn in at the gate. She was in its path, she realised immediately, but as she stepped aside another thought occurred to her. Who was driving the estate car? she wondered tensely. This was Joe's house. Could it be him?

It wasn't. It was a woman at the wheel, but despite her apprehension Olivia knew instantly who it was. *Mrs*

Castellano, she acknowledged incredulously. She'd only seen her picture once, but her resemblance to Joe—or, rather, his to her—made the identification unmistakable.

Olivia was trying to think of some way to introduce herself, when the woman stopped the car beside her and rolled down the window. 'Yes?' she said tersely. 'Can I help you?'

Olivia licked her lips. Having the initiative taken out of her hands had startled her somewhat, and she struggled to find something suitable to say. 'Um—is—is Mr Castellano here?' she asked lamely. 'Mr *Joe* Castellano? I'd like to see him if he is.'

'Joseph?'

Olivia groaned. Of course, his mother would call him Joseph. 'Yes—Joseph,' she agreed, rather weakly. 'Do you think you could tell him I'm here?'

Mrs Castellano frowned. 'Could I tell him *who's* here?' she asked pointedly, her eyes—darker eyes than Joe's, Olivia noticed—taking a brief inventory of Olivia's appearance.

'Oh—Olivia,' she said hurriedly. 'Olivia Pyatt. I—I met your son when I was working in—'

'You're—Olivia?'

The woman was staring at her disbelievingly now, and Olivia guessed that if she had heard of her she was thinking that she was not the type of woman her son would normally be attracted to. 'Yes,' she answered, feeling her colour deepening. 'Is he here? Joe, I mean. I really would like to speak to him.'

'Would you?' Mrs Castellano shook her head, and Olivia was convinced she was going to refuse her request. 'Well—' she shrugged her shoulders '—you'd better get in. I'll take you up to the house.'

Olivia stared at her. 'You will?'

'It's what you want, isn't it?' The woman arched an imperious brow that was so like her son's that Olivia caught her breath.

'Well—yes,' she muttered, and when the woman pushed

open the door she hurried round the car. 'Thank you. Thank you very much.'

'Don't thank me.' The woman sounded the horn again, and this time an elderly man appeared to open the gates. She nodded at him as they passed, and then gave Olivia another appraising look. 'I hope you're not going to tell Joseph any more lies,' she added coolly. 'He may be the head of the family, but to me he's just my eldest son.'

Olivia stared at her now. 'Lies?' she echoed defensively. 'I haven't told him any lies.'

'No?' Mrs Castellano looked sceptical. 'Then why did I get the impression that you had?'

Olivia blinked. 'What exactly did Joe tell you, Mrs Castellano?'

'I don't think that's any concern of yours.' Joe's mother spoke impulsively, and then seemed to think better of it. 'Oh—he hasn't talked to me, but I know my son.'

Olivia shook her head. 'I'm sorry.' A thought occurred to her. 'But perhaps it's not me who's upset him.' She hesitated. 'I expect you know of his—his friendship with Diane Haran?'

'The actress?' Mrs Castellano was scathing. 'Oh, she'd like to think Joseph was interested in her. But I'm afraid she'll have to be content with Mark instead.'

Olivia blinked. 'Mark?'

'My younger son,' prompted Joe's mother impatiently, and Olivia remembered the first morning she had spent at the Beverly Hills mansion, and Diane saying that Joe's brother was an actor, too. 'I don't approve of him getting involved with a married woman,' she went on irritably. 'Particularly as I'm fairly sure she only used the connection to get to Joseph.'

Olivia tried to absorb what she was hearing. Was this woman saying that Diane had been having an affair with Joe's brother, not with him?

'In Los Angeles, people will do anything for money,' Mrs Castellano continued, unaware of her guest's confusion. 'They're always looking for finance for their films, you know.'

Olivia didn't know what to say. She was trembling, as much with disbelief at what she had heard as with apprehension at seeing Joe again. 'But—Joe—Joseph is here, isn't he?' she ventured nervously.

'Yes, he's here,' declared his mother, somewhat unwillingly. 'I don't suppose you'd like to tell me why you've come?'

'I—need to see him,' said Olivia awkwardly. And then, remembering something else, she asked, 'Could you tell me how you knew my name?'

The older woman's lips twisted. 'I'm not a psychic, Miss Pyatt. Joseph has spoken to me about you. Though not this week, I must admit.' Her brows arched. 'But don't ask me to tell you in what context you were mentioned. Like you, I prefer to keep my feelings to myself.'

As they'd been speaking, Mrs Castellano had been driving along the twisting track up to the house, but it was only as they each fell silent that Olivia was able to take any notice of her surroundings. Tall pines, dwarf poplars and cyprus hedged the path with their branches, and the smell of resin drifted in through the estate car's windows.

Up close, the house was less intimidating. Olivia could now see that what she had thought was a parapet was really a widow's walk. But there were turrets, and a kind of round tower marked one corner of the building. And it was much older than the house at Malibu, with a fascinating aura of the past.

'It used to belong to a seafaring family,' remarked Mrs Castellano, noticing Olivia's interest in the house. 'In the days when the big clippers sailed to China. My husband bought the place in 1922.'

Olivia was getting out of the car. 'You live here?' she asked, unaware of the apprehension in her voice.

'Not since Giovanni died,' returned her hostess, with a wry expression. 'I live in the city. But I don't deny I worry about Joseph living here alone.'

Was that why she wanted Joe to marry Anna Fellini? Olivia wondered tensely, half afraid to dismiss the threat Diane had presented from her thoughts. But she was beginning to see that Richard had been mistaken about so many things; or perhaps he'd just chosen to interpret them that way.

Like that photograph, for example. What if it was of Mark Castellano and Diane? It would possibly explain why they'd chosen to go to San Diego. Mr and Mrs Castellano. Was she clutching at straws to think that Joe was too fastidious to do something like that?

'I expect Joseph's in the library,' his mother went on briskly, and Olivia realised how much she cared about her son. 'I won't ask Victor to announce you—not unless you want me to, of course?' She raised a questioning brow, nodding at Olivia's quick denial. 'I thought not.'

They entered the house by way of a charming entrance hall with a dark-stained staircase leading up on the right. The floor was polished wood with a hand-woven rug in the centre, and there were several seascapes and a magnificent barometer hanging on the panelled walls.

Through open, double-panelled doors on her left, Olivia could see a high-ceilinged living room, with long, square-cut windows, giving a delightful view of the bay. Tall cabinets, antique tables, and plenty of easy chairs and sofas strewn with cushions, gave the room a homely ambience, and it was this as much as anything that distinguished it from the house at Malibu.

This was where Joe *lived*, thought Olivia, with an involuntary shiver. This was his home in the truest sense of the word. She would have liked to spend a few moments absorbing that fact and holding it to her. But an older man had appeared through a door set beneath the stairs, his lined face breaking into a smile when he saw who one of his visitors was.

'Good morning, ma'am.' He greeted Joe's mother warmly. And, although he must have been curious as to her identity, he was too polite to ask who Olivia was. 'I didn't

know you were expected,' he added. 'Would you like me
to tell your son that you're here?'

'That won't be necessary, Victor,' said Mrs Castellano
firmly. 'Joseph isn't expecting me, but I think we'd like to
give him a surprise. This is Miss Pyatt, by the way. She's
a—friend of Joseph's. Tell me, is he in the library or holed
up in his den?'

'I believe he's in the library, Mrs Castellano,' said Victor
politely. Then, turning to Olivia, he said, 'Welcome to
Dragon's Rest, Miss Pyatt. Can I get you anything? A cup
of coffee or—?'

'*I'll* have an espresso, Victor,' broke in Joe's mother,
with another glance in Olivia's direction. 'I think Miss
Pyatt would prefer to see Joseph. Isn't that right?'

Olivia nodded her head a little energetically, and then,
realising it wasn't very polite, she managed a faint, 'Yes.'
But in all honesty she would have preferred to sit down
with Joe's mother and delay the moment when she would
have to face him. She was suddenly assaulted with the conviction that she shouldn't have come.

'Would you like me to—?' began Victor, but once again
Mrs Castellano interrupted him.

'I'll make sure Miss Pyatt finds the library,' she in-
structed him crisply. 'If you'll bring my coffee to the living
room, I'd be very grateful.'

'Yes, ma'am.'

Victor departed, not without some misgivings, Olivia
suspected, but he knew better than to offend his employer's
mother. 'Now,' she said, turning to the younger woman, 'I
trust you won't betray my confidence in you. If you go up
to the second floor, it's the first door on your right.'

In fact, Olivia reflected as she climbed the stairs on
slightly unsteady legs, she meant the first floor. Americans
called the ground floor the first floor, and therefore the next
floor up was the second. It made sense, she decided, aware
that she was trying to divert her fears. But she was so afraid
she'd made a terrible mistake.

She emerged onto a galleried landing, with a long corridor leading in the opposite direction that was panelled with richly polished oak like the hall below. The walls here were hung with miniatures of sailing ships, and a brass lantern set on a semicircular table reminded her of Victorian lamps she'd seen in England.

The door Mrs Castellano had indicated was leather-studded and imposing. Like the panelling and the pictures, it reminded her of how old the house was. But beautifully maintained, she conceded, once again delaying her entrance. Everything about this place spelled old money and affluence.

She realised that if she waited any longer Joe's mother might come out of the living room and see her hovering on the landing. Or Joe himself could have heard his mother's arrival and surely then he'd feel obliged to greet his guest. With a jerky movement, she grazed her knuckles on the leather, before summoning all her courage and giving an audible tap.

'Come in.'

It was his voice, albeit it didn't sound very welcoming, and Olivia turned the handle of the door and stepped inside the room before she could change her mind. But even the effort of opening the door had exhausted her, and she held onto the handle for support.

'I heard the car,' said Joe's voice impatiently, but although Olivia scanned the book-lined room she couldn't see where he was. 'You don't have to keep coming here, Mom. I don't need company. I'll be perfectly all right if you'll give me a little space.'

Olivia blinked, and carefully closed the door behind her. Where was he? she wondered, leaning back against the panels, as if she was afraid to move away. He wasn't sitting at the desk or examining any of the leather-bound volumes on the shelves that gave the room its distinctive odour, and she was frowning in confusion when a high-backed chair that had been facing the windows swung about.

His expression when he saw her wasn't encouraging. It was obvious he'd been expecting to see his mother, and he

stared at Olivia with narrow-lidded eyes. He didn't even
get to his feet; he just sat there gazing as if at an apparition.
Then, shaking his head, he raked back his hair with an
unsteady hand.

Olivia swallowed. Although she could see his face, his
eyes were in shadow, and, realising it was up to her to say
something, she murmured, 'Hello, Joe.' And then, when he
still didn't speak, she forced a smile to her lips. 'I—I guess
you're surprised to see me, aren't you?'

'You could say that.' His voice was harsh and unfriendly.
His hands closed on the chair arms. 'Where's Rick—
Richard? Does he know you're here?'

'Of course not.' Olivia was defensive. She was not sufficiently sure of herself to dissemble in any way. 'I—as far
as I know, he's still in England. What he chooses to do
doesn't have anything to do with me.'

'Don't lie.' Joe moved now, pushing himself to his feet
and stepping away from the chair. 'What happened? Didn't
it work out as you anticipated? Did he get cold feet at the
thought of giving up all that dough?'

Olivia swallowed. 'I don't know what you're talking
about,' she said unsteadily. She stared at him, noticing how
stark and drawn his face looked in the light. If she didn't
know better, she'd have thought he'd suffered some kind
of bereavement. 'I've told you, what Richard does is nothing to do with me.'

Joe's lips compressed. 'So what was he doing accompanying you to England?' he demanded. 'I notice you don't
deny that that's where he went.'

'No. How could I?' Olivia shook her head. 'But I didn't
know he was going to take that flight.'

'Really?' He sounded sceptical.

'Yes, really.' Olivia pressed the palms of her hands together and moved away from the door. 'I couldn't believe
it when he came and sat beside me. But I should have
known Diane would tell him which flight I intended to
take.'

'Diane?'

'Yes, Diane,' said Olivia, a little uncomfortably. She licked her lips. 'I suppose she told you, too.'

'Diane told me nothing,' retorted Joe roughly. 'I haven't spoken to her for several days.'

'But—'

He frowned. 'Go on.'

'But—the night before I left—' She coloured. 'I was told Diane stayed with you at—at Malibu.'

'*We* were together the night before you left,' he reminded her harshly. 'How the hell was I supposed to be in two places at once?'

Olivia blinked. 'But Bonnie said—'

'Yes?' His eyes were cold. 'What did Bonnie say to convince you?'

'Well—that Diane was staying with you at—at Malibu.'

'She actually said that: that Diane and I were staying together?' he exclaimed savagely. 'Oh, come on, Olivia. You'll have to do better than that.'

'She did.' Olivia was desperate. 'I swear it.' She tried to remember the exact words. 'She said she was staying with Mr Castellano. What was I supposed to think?'

Joe's expression was remote. 'So that's why you invited Richard to go to England with you. You thought Diane was with me, so what the hell, you'd get your revenge?'

'No!' Olivia caught her breath. 'Oh, this is ridiculous! If you won't listen to reason, I might as well go.'

A sob rising in her throat, she turned towards the door, but before she could get it open Joe said, 'Wait!' With a muffled oath, he crossed the floor to halt in front of her. 'Just tell me why you came, hmm? I have to know.'

'Why?' Now it was Olivia's turn to be awkward. 'Why should I tell you anything? You're not going to believe me.'

'Perhaps I will,' he said harshly, his eyes dark and tormented. And, because she so badly wanted to reassure him, she gave in.

'I—I wanted to know if—if what happened between us meant anything to you,' she admitted jerkily. 'Richard—' She used her ex-husband's name reluctantly, but his part in her decision had to be explained. 'Richard said that he'd spoken to you after—after I went down to the Bistro. What he told you wasn't true; I have no desire to live with him again.'

Joe's eyes narrowed. 'But you told me you'd spoken to him.' He made an impatient gesture. 'That night, before I phoned, you said he'd been on the line.'

'He was.' Olivia was trembling. 'But I told him I didn't want to see him. I had no idea that later on he'd told you the opposite.'

Joe frowned. 'But you had left the suite, hadn't you?'

'Yes. Because you were asleep, and I wanted to get something to eat.' She sighed, tugging nervously at her braid. 'Oh, you might as well know all of it. I was frightened I was falling in love with you, and I told myself that if I had something to eat I wouldn't feel so hollow inside.'

Joe's eyes darkened. 'Are you serious?' He lifted one hand and tilted her chin up to his face.

'I wouldn't have flown over five thousand miles if I hadn't been serious,' she said honestly. 'Oh, Joe, I'm so sorry. But I had to tell you how I felt.'

Joe's fingers caressed the skin behind her ear. 'And how do you feel?' he asked huskily.

Olivia flushed now. 'I care about you,' she muttered with a downbent head.

'You care about me?' he echoed, using his other hand to force her to look up at him again. 'Like—does love came into that? I'd really like to know.'

Olivia groaned. 'You know it does,' she said hotly, half afraid he was playing with her. She took a breath that mingled his warmth and maleness with her surroundings. 'I know I'm nothing like Diane, but I can't help that.'

'Thank God,' he said in a curiously strangled voice, pulling her towards him. He buried his face in the hollow of her shoulder, and she felt his teeth against the skin of her neck. 'I guess it's my fault for letting you think that Diane meant something to me. I like her, sure; but she's really my brother's playmate, not mine.'

Olivia was shaking now at this admission. 'You—you mean you and she aren't—weren't—having an affair?'

Joe lifted his head and bestowed a warm kiss on her parted lips. 'No,' he said, when she was weak with languor. 'Mark introduced us, and I guess she saw me as a more lucrative source of cash.'

Olivia shook her head helplessly. 'I think you underestimate yourself,' she said, sliding her arms around his waist. 'Oh, Joe, are you really pleased to see me? You're not just being kind because I'm here?'

Joe's exhalation was fervent. 'Are you crazy?' he asked, sliding his hands down her spine to cup her bottom and bring her against him. His instinctive arousal pushed against her stomach, and she looked up at him tremulously. 'I didn't know what love was until I met you. Then, I wasn't sure that I wanted to know.'

'Because of what Richard said?'

'Partly. And because I was angry. I couldn't believe you'd walked out on me, and his call was just the final straw. Then, when I went down to the lobby and saw you, you were signing someone's copy of your book. I convinced myself you were more interested in selling books than pleasing me.'

'Joe—'

'I know, I know.' He pulled her over to the chair where he'd been sitting and drew her onto his knee. 'It was childish, but I couldn't help it. I was so jealous I'd have believed anything of you that night.'

Olivia cupped his face in her hands. 'You were jealous?' she exclaimed disbelievingly.

'You'd better believe it,' he told her roughly, sliding his hands beneath her shirt. 'I just wanted to get away, but I couldn't go to the house at Malibu because I'd said Mark could use it. So I chartered a flight and flew back here.'

'Oh, Joe...' She nuzzled her face into his neck as his hands explored her, finding the strap of her bra and releasing it with a satisfying little ping. 'I love you. I didn't know how I was going to live without you.' She hesitated. 'It's ironic but if it hadn't been for Richard I wouldn't be here.'

His hands stilled. 'Why not?' he asked, and although his expression was tense she knew she had to go on.

'Because I guessed—I *hoped*—it was because of what he'd told you that you didn't try to see me again. When I got on the plane, I had no hope of ever coming back.'

Joe's expression softened. 'In that case, I suppose I ought to thank him. Even if I wanted to kill him until a few minutes ago.' His hands gripped her waist and moved her until she was straddling his body. 'God, you can't know how good that feels.'

'I think I can,' she breathed, leaning in to him and caressing his mouth with her tongue. She put her hand down between them and stroked the outline of his manhood. 'Does this mean you want me to stay?'

'Try and get away,' he told her hoarsely, his hands slipping beneath her skirt now to find the yielding waistband of her panties. 'Just—let me—' His breath quickened as he unfastened the button of his jeans, and she caught her breath as she realised what he planned to do.

'What about your mother?' she protested, even as she did what she could to assist him, and Joe offered a sound of anguish at her words.

'I don't think she'll disturb us,' he assured her huskily. 'She knows what an unmitigated bastard I've been since I got back.'

'Because of me?' asked Olivia faintly, hardly daring to believe what he was saying.

'Because of you,' he agreed with feeling, tearing the silk a little as he eased into her heat. 'God, it seems a lifetime since we were together.'

'For me, too,' she whispered against his ear. 'Um—your mother said you'd mentioned my name to her.'

'I did,' he agreed, biting the lobe of her ear. 'After we'd spent that afternoon together, I knew I wanted you. But as Diane was convinced you still cared about Richard I wasn't certain you weren't just using me to make him jealous.'

'Using you...' Olivia's breath escaped on a sob as he moved inside her. 'Oh, Joe, I'm so glad I came back.'

'So am I,' he told her achingly as his fingers found her, and her senses swam as her feelings soared away...

EPILOGUE

OLIVIA's biography of Diane Haran was published to critical acclaim the following year. To her surprise, Diane had chosen not to change her biographer, even though by then she knew all about Olivia and Joe. But after meeting Mark Castellano, and discovering he was a younger, less intense version of his brother, Olivia decided she was hedging her bets. Diane was philosophical in some ways, and Mark was still a Castellano, after all.

But he was also a much less serious individual than his sibling, and although he was not averse to riding on Diane's coat-tails as an actor Olivia suspected he wouldn't want to settle down for some considerable time. It wasn't her concern, really, except insofar as Richard and Diane were separating. Richard never did produce the photograph, and Joe surmised Diane had paid him off.

Olivia wrote most of the biography after she and Joe returned from their honeymoon. They'd spent the weeks before the wedding arranging for Olivia's personal possessions to be transferred to the States. They'd also paid a flying visit to see her parents in Rotorua, and arranged for them to break their journey home in San Francisco, so that Olivia's father could be there to give her away.

It had been a whirlwind courtship but Olivia had loved every minute of it. She didn't really care what they did or where they went so long as they were together. Even Henry had settled down in his new surroundings, terrorising the neighbourhood's bird population from his favourite spot among the leaves of an old acacia.

Mrs Castellano—or Lucia, as she'd suggested Olivia should call her—had proved endlessly supportive, taking over the organisation of the wedding, which was to be in June, and welcoming the Pyatts into her home. There was no point, she'd said, in them returning to England before the wedding. She'd suggested an extension of their holiday, and offered her house as somewhere they might like to stay.

'It's just as well you've set the date,' she'd remarked to Olivia one afternoon, just a couple of weeks before the wedding. They had been studying catalogues of table decorations, making their final decisions over what flowers to choose. 'It's nicer to have the ceremony before you begin to show.'

Olivia, who had been studying a centrepiece of lilies and flame orchids, had looked at her future mother-in-law in surprise. 'Before what begins to show?' she asked uncomprehendingly. And then, as the realisation hit her, she said, 'You can't be serious!'

'Come on, Livvy.' Joe's mother had taken to calling her that, and she found it rather sweet. 'I thought of pretending I hadn't noticed, but I'm so excited, I can't keep it to myself. Doesn't Joseph know yet? Is that why you've kept it a secret for so long?'

Olivia didn't know what to say. She'd never dreamt that she might have conceived Joe's baby. Indeed, she'd lived for so long believing she'd never have a baby that any symptoms she'd noticed she'd attributed to something else.

'Nobody knows,' she said now dazedly. '*I* didn't know, until you mentioned it.' She swallowed, running a nervous hand across her abdomen. 'Do you think it's true?'

Lucia gave a knowing smile, dimples appearing in her cheeks. 'I'd say it was a definite possibility,' she murmured softly. 'Oh, my dear, when you turned pale at the sight of last night's oysters, I think I knew for certain then.'

Olivia shook her head. 'I had no idea,' she admitted honestly, and then explained why she'd been so unperceptive. She closed her eyes for a moment. 'Oh, God, I told Joe I couldn't have children. What is he going to think?'

'If I know my son, I'm fairly sure he'll be delighted,' Lucia assured her firmly. 'But thank you for the insight into my son's feelings for you. Knowing how much he's always said he wanted a family, he must love you very much.'

And Joe, when she told him, was delighted. 'But I thought you said—' he began, and she put a finger across his mouth.

'That was just another of Richard's lies,' she said, nestling closer to him. And then, changing the subject, she asked, 'Do you think we should tell my parents or not?'

The first draft of *Naked Instinct* was finished in October, and Diane, who was on location in Louisiana, had very few comments to make. Apart from approving the manuscript, and the title, she gave Olivia credit for writing it so quickly. And wished her luck in finding a publisher to take it on.

In fact, Olivia's own publisher was delighted to receive the manuscript from Kay Goldsmith, and the book itself was published just six months after Joe and Olivia's daughter was born.

'Two productions in one year,' murmured Joe one warm September evening, watching Olivia feed baby Virginia with possessive eyes. 'Can I make a request that next year you devote time to your husband? I love my daughter, but I'd also very much like some time with my wife—alone.'

Looking For More Romance?

Visit Romance.net

Check in daily for these and other exciting features:

Hot off the press

View all current titles, and purchase them on-line.

What do the stars have in store for you?

Horoscope

Hot deals

Exclusive offers available only at Romance.net

Plus, don't miss our interactive quizzes, contests and bonus gifts.

PWEB

Rebellious, bold and...
a father!

THE AUSTRALIANS

Stories of romance Australian-style, guaranteed to
fulfill that sense of adventure!

This May 1999 look for
Taming a Husband
by Elizabeth Duke

Jake Thorn has never been one to settle down. He couldn't
stay with Lexie, even though his heart yearned to, and he
struck out across the continent before she could tell the
daddy-to-be the big news. Now, determined to give love
another chance, Jake has returned—and is shocked to find
himself a father!

*The Wonder from Down Under: where spirited women win
the hearts of Australia's most independent men!*

Available May 1999
at your favorite retail outlet.

HARLEQUIN®
Makes any time special ™

Coming Next Month

HARLEQUIN PRESENTS®

THE BEST HAS JUST GOTTEN BETTER!

#2025 THE PERFECT LOVER Penny Jordan
(A Perfect Family)
While recovering from the emotional blow of unrequited love, Louise Crighton had rebounded into Gareth Simmonds's passionate arms. They'd shared a whirlwind holiday romance... but now their paths were about to cross again....

#2026 THE MILLIONAIRE'S MISTRESS Miranda Lee
(Presents Passion)
When Justine waltzed into Marcus's office, making it clear she'd do *anything* for a loan, he assumed she was just a gold-digger. He still desired her though, and she became his mistress. Then he realized how wrong he'd been....

#2027 MARRIAGE ON THE EDGE Sandra Marton
(The Barons)
Gage Baron's wife, Natalie, had just left him, and the last thing he wanted to do was go to his father's birthday party. But it was an opportunity to win back his wife; his father expected Natalie to attend the party and share Gage's bed!

#2028 THE PLAYBOY'S BABY Mary Lyons
(Expecting!)
As a successful career girl, Samantha thought she could handle a no-strings relationship with her old flame, Matthew Warner. But Sam had broken both the rules: she'd fallen in love with the sexy playboy *and* fallen pregnant!

#2029 GIORDANNI'S PROPOSAL Jacqueline Baird
Beth suspected that Italian tycoon Dex Giordanni had only asked her to marry him to settle a family score. She broke off the engagement, but Dex wasn't taking no for an answer; if she wasn't his fiancée, she'd have to be his mistress!

#2030 THE SEDUCTION GAME Sara Craven
Tara Lyndon had almost given up on men until she met gorgeous hunk Adam Barnard. Unfortunately, this perfect man also had a "perfect fiancée" waiting in the wings. There was only one thing to do to get her man: seduce him!